SPELL SEARCH

MERRY MAGIC BOOK 4

SHELLEY RUSSELL NOLAN

CHAPTER 1

A key clanged in the door lock and Merry stuffed her grandmother's journal down beside the cushion on her wing backed chair and jumped to her feet. Back to the crackling fire, hands clenched into fists, she kept her eyes on the door as the handle turned. It was hard to tell the time, in a room with no windows or clock, but they shouldn't be bringing her dinner yet. It wasn't long since her morning guards had watched on as a servant brought her lunch and collected the tray containing the remains of Merry's breakfast. The door to her prison opened, and four enforcers stepped inside.

Four?

Usually there were two, both ready to immobilise her in a split second if she attempted to escape. She'd considered it, but as well as being armed with their telekinetic ability, the enforcers who guarded her carried swords. All she had was her wooden staff. Not even close to a fair match.

As the four enforcers fanned around the room, leaving the door open behind them, Merry eyed them warily.

Adrian Irvine was one of the enforcers, and this was the first time she had seen anyone she knew since the day she woke to find herself locked in a gilded cage. Gabriel Fairweather had been sleeping in the very chair she had just been sitting in, waiting to deliver the bad news. To save her life, he had brought her to the one place he had promised to never bring her against her will; the guild tower.

It was the same tower in which her grandmother had been imprisoned for over twenty years.

Adrian's stance was rigid, jaw clenched as he stared back at her. None of the enforcers had ever answered her questions, but maybe he would. He might know how Gabriel was doing, and if he was still locked up in a room on the same floor as Merry. He might have word of Ellen and Sadie. It had been a week since she'd woken from the coma brought on by magical exhaustion.

A week of not knowing if her friends were all right.

A week of being cut off from her magic, the muffling in her head a constant reminder.

Merry pulled her thoughts from everything she was missing out on and opened her mouth to ask Adrian about Ellen. A flash of purple caught her eye and her gaze snapped back to the open door.

A Spirit mage stood in the entrance, purple robe shimmering in the light.

The mage's face was thin and stern. She was tall, her robe coming to just below her knees and hemmed in silver thread. From the rigid set of her features she was not accustomed to smiling, and the look she gave Merry was cold and cutting.

'You are to come with me.' The mage's tone was as chilling as her gaze. 'Do not attempt to use magic or you will be neutralised.'

Merry's heart raced at the thought of leaving the room. All her things were here. Her staff and the spell box containing the elemental charms she had so far collected, were here, as well as the amethyst and journal that had belonged to her grandmother, found in a hidden compartment in the brick wall behind the heavy timber wardrobe. The compartment contained a slice of magic; one she had yet to figure out how to use to her advantage.

'Where are we going?' She would not leave her things behind if she was about to exchange one prison for another.

The mage waved a hand and Adrian left his post by the wall and stepped closer to Merry, hands raised.

Immediately, a tight band settled around Merry's throat, constricting her breathing, his telekinetic ability not affected by the ward that prevented Merry from accessing her elemental magic.

'Do not speak unless you are given permission to do

so.' The mage whipped around, robe flaring out behind her as she stepped into the hall. The band around Merry's throat eased, even as a new band settled around her body, pinning her arms to her sides.

'Walk,' said Adrian, glowering as he indicated with his head for her to move ahead of him.

When Merry failed to move, a hard shove in the middle of her back had her stumbling forward.

'Branstone. Enough.' Adrian shifted his glower to an enforcer on the other side of the room. 'I will deal with her.'

The enforcer inclined his head. 'As you wish, Master Irvine.'

Adrian faced Merry once more, and this time his gaze was less of a glower and more of a plea. 'You must come with us, Miss Meadows.' The band around her middle lessened and he waved a hand towards the doorway behind him.

She shot a glance at the other enforcer, Branstone, who appeared eager to have a chance to use his tele-kinetic ability to shove her again despite Adrian's order. The other two enforcers watched on with equally deter-mined expressions.

Merry lifted her head and did her best to ignore her armed escort as she stepped towards the door. If she was being taken to another prison, she would find a way to escape and retrieve her belongings. Besides, if they were taking her away from the prison floor, she would have access to her magic again. She would finally be able to contact Sadie telepathically.

One way or another, she would use this as an opportunity to escape.

The Spirit mage was waiting outside the room, at the end of a long hallway, arms crossed in front of her chest. As soon as the four enforcers took up positions to the sides and back of Merry, she set off down the hall at a fast pace. With enforcers at her back, keeping an equally fast pace, Merry had to step quickly to avoid being run over. Adrian was to her left and he cast a quick glance her way.

Would he attempt to stop her when she made her escape? Rebuking a junior enforcer for unnecessary force was one thing, aiding and abetting an escapee another. She could not rely on his help.

The hallway was well lit, showing a number of closed doors on either side. It appeared the guild had plenty of accommodations for witches and mages who refused to bow down to their rule. Gabriel could be locked behind any one of these doors, but there was no telling which one.

The quick pace continued and at the end of the hallway Merry was ushered through a large wooden door. This led to the landing for a narrow stone stairwell that spiralled downward. It was cold in the stairwell, and Merry rubbed her arms at the reminder that winter was fast approaching and time running out to stop witch hunters entering Tirana. She had to escape and to get the last two charms for her transportation spell, to prevent that from happening.

As she reached the next floor, the muffling in Merry's head vanished and her body thrummed and pulsed.

Her magic was back.

Merry instantly reached out to Sadie, even as she drew on her magic, revelling in the feel of it as it filled her body and chased away the chill encasing the stairwell. *Can you hear me?*

Merry! Finally, you...

A sharp pain speared Merry's temples, and Sadie's mental voice cut off. The Spirit mage whirled around, making the enforcers halt mid-step, one of them stumbling into Merry.

'I said no magic.' The mage held up a hand, palm facing Merry as the pain in her head intensified. 'Do you understand?'

Pain tightened its grip on Merry's head, even as a wave of goosebumps coursing over her skin told her the mage was working some kind of spell. Merry clamped her jaw to keep from making a sound, though she could not prevent tears forming in her eyes. She gave a nod.

For a moment, the Spirit mage just stared at her, the pain unrelenting, a vise that squeezed and squeezed until Merry was ready to scream. Then the mage lowered her hand and the pain stopped as abruptly as it had begun.

Merry sucked air in through clenched teeth. She

wanted to sag to her knees, clutch her head, and find a dark corner to hide in. What the mage had done to her paled in comparison to when Mage Fowler had attacked her mind, but it still left vestiges of pain throbbing in her temples in time with her pulse. She forced herself to remain upright, glaring at the mage as she lifted her chin.

The mage did not react, other than to indicate for the enforcers to continue on. All the while her lips were moving with no sound emerging. Merry did not hear from Sadie again, so the mage's spell must have been to stop the familiar from telepathically communicating with her.

After so long without being able to talk to the little black cat, to have that brief moment of contact only to have it ripped away from her so quickly stung. Merry knew she must find a way to get through the block the mage had created. Magic thrummed all around her, through her, making her ache to use it. But the Spirit mage would know as soon as she did and cut her off. The pain in her head had faded, but she did not want a repeat.

Instead, she opened herself up, trying to sift through her impressions of the thrumming in her body. It was similar to what she had felt when she was at the Earth, Air and Water focal points, so it had to be the Spirit focal point she was reacting to. The guild tower was built directly above it. But there was something else she could sense; something that filled her with yearning, made her increase her pace so that now it was the enforcers having to keep up with her as she sensed she was getting closer.

They travelled down numerous floors, with no doors branching off the stone landings, until they reached one that had a wooden door reinforced with thick bands of black metal. The Spirit mage produced a key, murmuring a silent spell as she placed it in the lock. There was a soft click and the door swung open. The enforcers ushered Merry through, and she stepped into a huge hall with marble columns supporting the weight of an arched ceiling carved in intricate swirls.

Dozens of people in a multitude of coloured garments thronged throughout the large space and they all stopped to stare at Merry and the enforcers as she was led towards them. A few of them wore drab clothing that suggested they were servants or visitors to the tower, but most of them had to be witches in training to become mages as they wore coloured long-sleeved dresses or tunics and trousers. There were over a dozen enforcers standing in the middle of the space and they were in the process of ushering people aside as Merry was marched into their midst, their footsteps echoing on the tiled floor.

Muted whispers and dark stares were sent Merry's way and made her wonder what these people knew of her. Not that it mattered. The enforcers cleared the path, and she was marched through the end arch and into a space that was just as intimidating if on a slightly smaller scale.

The arches in here framed a raised dais and a collection of timber pews, while colourful tapestries with images representing each of the magical elements lined the walls. It reminded Merry of medieval churches she had seen in history books, though there were no stained-glass windows. Twice as many people as those who had occupied the large hall were seated on the pews, all of them in mage robes. Many of them twisted around to stare at Merry as she was ushered down the centre aisle to a space in front of the dais, and a quiet murmur followed in her wake.

The hall was rounded, and she got the sense it was in the centre of the tower. The thrumming from beneath her was stronger here, so they had to be directly over the Spirit focal point. But it was not that which called to her now. In the centre of the dais sat a marble pedestal. On top of it, swathed in a shimmering purple cloth, was a round shape the size of a bowling ball.

Merry could not take her eyes from it, every atom in her body telling her to climb the dais, sweep aside the cloth and lay hands on whatever lay beneath it. The enforcers would try to stop her, as would the Spirit mage, but none of that mattered. She had to have it. Whatever it was.

She had tensed, ready to call on her magic and damn the consequences, when she heard her name being called by a familiar voice. With a shudder, she tore her gaze away from the dais and looked sideways.

Gabriel now stood to the left of the dais, a Spirit mage and four enforcers surrounding him. He was wearing his blue and white mage robe, looking as handsome and elegant as ever, though there was tension in the way he stood. It appeared he was just as much a prisoner as she was, even though his aunt led the mage guild.

Despite the tension in his body, his gaze was warm as he looked at Merry, a smile curving his lips. He took a step towards her, only to be pulled up short.

He cast a wry glance at the enforcer directly to his left. 'I just want to talk to her. I'm not trying to escape.'

The enforcer looked to the mage watching over Gabriel.

The mage frowned. 'No talking between prisoners.'

The enforcer gave a nod and waved his hand towards Gabriel. The young mage's body stiffened, and he was yanked backwards. Features contorted, he gasped for air while beside him the enforcer clenched his fists.

'Leave him alone. He didn't do anything wrong,' said Merry, surging forward. Adrian stepped into her path, and she felt her momentum slow as invisible bonds wrapped around her lower body.

'Don't make it worse for him.'

The words were tersely spoken, in a tone so low Merry doubted anyone else would have heard them. She shot a startled glance at Adrian, and then subsided at the concerned look he directed towards Gabriel. She did not want to make the situation worse for him when all he had done was try to help her. Adrian gave her a curt nod, and the invisible bonds holding her in place eased, though they did not disappear entirely.

On the other side of the hall, the enforcer immobilising Gabriel stepped back and the young mage appeared to be able to breathe more easily. She suspected he was still bound in some way to ensure he could be immediately neutralised if he were to step out of line again. The injustice of the situation burned through Merry. This was wrong. Gabriel should not have been punished because of her. He was a good man, one who wanted what was best for all the people of Tirana. His aunt had to see that. Merry would make her see that if she got the chance.

Movement near the dais pulled her attention away from Gabriel and she twisted her head to see a dark-haired woman emerging from an alcove to the right, posture rigid and head held high. The imposing woman wore a purple mage robe with thick bands of blue, green, orange and white around the hem. With purposeful strides, the mage ascended the stairs leading up to the dais and took her place beside the pedestal. The woman's expression was haughty and cold as she smoothed down her shimmering robe while silence descended over the hall.

The silence stretched on, no one daring to move, as the woman's penetrating gaze focused on Merry. Top lip curling with disdain, she narrowed her eyes and said, 'So, you are Meredith Meadows; the witch who believes guild law does not apply to her. Your traitorous grandmother felt the same way and was exiled for it. You will not be given the opportunity to spread your filthy lies and foster unrest among my loyal mages.' Here her gaze flicked to Gabriel and then laser focused on Merry again. 'I am Ophelia Fairweather, leader of the mage guild, and you are here to be brought to account for breaking guild law.'

Merry sucked in a breath, but before she could say anything in her defence, Gabriel called out, 'This is not Merry's world. The guild can't hold her accountable for breaking laws she didn't even know existed.'

At his words, a muted mutter once again arose from the mages seated in the pews behind Merry.

Ophelia did not shift her gaze from Merry as she waved a hand, and Gabriel was silenced once more.

'Ignorance is no excuse. Regardless of where she was born… Merry… is of the Meadows bloodline and, along with her magical ability, she has inherited the rights and responsibilities her grandmother chose to throw away; to join the guild and train to use her magic for the good of Tirana.'

Merry snorted. 'For the good of the guild, you mean. You don't care about the people of Tirana unless they are potential mages.' Even as she said the words, she expected to be cut off. From everything she had heard about the guild leader, Ophelia Fairweather would not countenance anyone contradicting her. She had already silenced her own nephew. A quick glance showed Gabriel was standing rigid, hands grasping at the invisible bonds used by the enforcers guarding him to keep him silent and still. The bonds around Merry did not tighten, so she continued to speak her mind.

'Your restrictions on how mages are to use their magic are wrong. Innocent people are dying because they can't afford the exorbitant prices you force guild mages to charge.' Merry would never forget the face of the woman whose baby girl was doomed to die in Pillingston, all because she couldn't pay for a mage healer. This was why her grandmother and other mages like her had turned against the teachings of the guild. It was not because they were traitors, but because they truly did care about all the people of Tirana.

Ophelia Fairweather's nostrils flared. 'You, who have spent mere weeks in Tirana, dare to lecture me on how the guild should be run?'

'Someone needs to,' said Merry, with a toss of her head. 'You've been holed up in this tower for so long you've clearly lost touch with the real world.'

The guild leader's expression darkened, hands clenching into fists. A wave of energy washed over Merry, making her reel, even as her sense of the Spirit focal point strengthened. She braced herself for whatever Ophelia was about to do as goosebumps erupted over her entire body. But nothing happened.

On the dais, Ophelia visibly relaxed, giving Merry a

sly smile. 'Running a guild of this nature is no easy task, but perhaps you think you could do a better job. Is that it? You wish to be the ruler of the guild?'

Merry shook her head. 'I just want to go home. Ever since I came here I've been caught up in one disaster after another. None of them would have happened if you and your precious guild were prepared to listen to the people, and realise witches are just as valuable as mages, and that those without magic need to be protected.'

Ellen was not a strong witch, but she spent her days trying to help people, unlike the mage strength healers who were oath bound to follow guild rules. Surely most of them would prefer to be out there healing the sick, and not just those who could pay guild prices.

'Very well then,' said Ophelia, that sly smile still on her lips. 'I will give you the opportunity you seek; to rule the guild and determine how mages should ply their trade.'

Merry blinked rapidly as she tried to process the turn around. 'Ah, what?'

'As my nephew so eloquently stated, you were not born here, so perhaps I was too hasty in condemning you for your grandmother's actions. As recompense, I will allow you to prove me wrong. Join the guild. Train to use your magic under the guidance of learned mages. Study hard, and one day you may rise to the role of guild leader and have the chance to mould the shape of the guild and all Tirana.'

With the flair of a magician unveiling their show stopping act, Ophelia reached out and pulled the purple cloth off the pedestal beside her. Eyes wide, breath stilled, Merry stared at the heartstone that was revealed. It was the size of a man's head, the purple and blues swirling in a mesmerising fashion.

She could not tear her gaze from it.

It called to her, singing through her veins, inducing her to step forward and place her hands on it. The song reminded her of one she'd heard Alicia, Mistress of Songs, sing when she had bound Merry's heartstone to her after she'd chased Lord Andel out of the Cavern of Heart Songs.

But she didn't move. She couldn't move with the invisible bonds Adrian had placed around her to keep her from reaching Gabriel earlier. These were now tightening, making it hard to breathe. Or was her breathlessness caused by the yearning to touch the heartstone? It was so beautiful. It was everything she had ever wanted and more. Nothing mattered. Nothing existed. Only the heartstone.

Dimly, Merry realised Ophelia was still talking to her. The words jarred, striking discordant notes into the heartstone's song.

'You will never get a better offer. Place your hands on the heartstone and swear an oath to obey guild law, and you will be set free to become a valued member of the guild.'

Merry ached to do as Ophelia said, to lay her hands

on the heartstone. Not to make any stupid oath, but just to touch it, caress it. The longer she stared at it, the stronger the desire to touch it grew, and the thrumming in her body increased tenfold. Despite the memory of the pain the Spirit mage had inflicted last time Merry tried to use her magic, she reached deep within herself to find her Earth magic. She would do whatever it took to touch the heartstone, even if that meant bringing the entire guild tower down around her.

Her Earth magic did not respond, and neither did Air or Water when she tried them. What was going on? Why was none of it working?

She turned sideways and saw that her Spirit mage guard was still muttering her silent spell, blocking Merry's magic.

How was she supposed to get to the stone without using it?

The song it produced swelled in the air.

The song.

Merry opened her mouth, not caring that she had a terrible singing voice as she prepared to sing the stone's song. Something covered her mouth. She reached up to tear it away, but her fingers found nothing. Yet she could not make a sound.

'Merry.' Adrian's harsh whisper pulled her back to herself, and she tore her gaze away from the heartstone to stare at the enforcer. His brow was creased, concern in his hazel gaze.

He had never called her by her first name before.

Awareness returned, and Merry blanched at what she had wanted to do. She would have placed her hands on the stone that would bind her magic to the guild; a guild ruled by Ophelia Fairweather. She remembered Ellen telling her of rumours it could bind people against their will. And she had been eager, obsessed even, with touching it.

She swallowed heavily and straightened her back, turning away from Adrian when the invisible gag vanished.

Then she looked Ophelia Fairweather in the eye and said the words that would doom her.

'I would rather spend the rest of my life locked in the tower than swear an oath to obey you.'

CHAPTER 2

*J*n the stunned silence that met her words, Merry felt deep inside her to block out the siren call of the heartstone. She refused to look at it, focusing her gaze on the maddening guild leader instead. If this was the only chance she would get, then she would make sure she was heard. Ophelia might not be prepared to listen, but the hall was filled with mages. Maybe one of them would be able to make their leader see sense.

'You're as bad as Lord Andel, forcing people with magic to swear an oath to obey you. He has hundreds of witches already enslaved and dozens more captured. If he finds a way to get more heartstones the rest will also be enslaved. And when he has enough of them, he's going to come here with his army, knock you off your dais, and proclaim himself king.'

'A bunch of field witches hardly constitutes an army.'

Amusement threaded through Ophelia's voice. 'No matter how many of them Lord Andel has managed to round up, they will be no match for trained mages.'

'Trained mages like the ones that poisoned half of Marshland Province, on Lord Andel's orders?' Merry shook her head. How could the woman be so blind? She had to see that her restrictions were destabilising Tirana.

'Trained they may be, but a few rogues were no match for the guild mages I sent to take care of the problem. Marshland is poison free, because of the guild.'

Heat flushed through Merry, her anger serving to further block the heartstone's call. 'Are you kidding me? Guild mages helped, but so did many of the Water witches in Marshland, including Lady Beatrice. If it wasn't for them, the poison would be spreading through all of Tirana.'

Ophelia inclined her head. 'Witches can prove useful on occasion, but it will be guild mages who turn back any attempt by Lord Andel, or anyone else, to reinstate a monarchy. Not witches.' No amusement coloured her words this time. Her voice was steely; resolute.

Despite knowing nothing she said would change Ophelia's mind, Merry pushed for some inkling that the guild leader possessed any humanity. 'Don't you care that Earth witches were forced to illegally mine heartstones for Andel, working until they were beyond exhausted? Or that witches in Andelmine Province are being starved into submission? Britta. Gregor. Rupert.

Catherine.' She placed careful emphasis on each name, desperate to get Ophelia to see them as people, her voice shaking as she said the last one. She would never forget the horrible way Catherine had succumbed to the insidious torture and agreed to swear the oath to Lord Andel.

'It is regrettable that Andel has employed such dubious tactics in his ridiculous effort to puff up his own importance. If you truly care about the fate of those field witches, you will take the oath and train to be a mage under my guidance,' said Ophelia, showing no sign she was affected by the list of names.

Merry wanted to shake her, to reach out and make her understand. 'They need help now. Not in however many years it would take me to become a mage. If you're so convinced your guild mages are more than a match for Andel's forces, then mount a rescue. Go to Andelmine and free the captured witches.'

'A campaign of that nature would be foolhardy, leaving the tower shorthanded when we need every mage here to ensure it does not fall into enemy hands. The guild tower is the heart of Tirana. It must be defended at all costs.' As she spoke, Ophelia leaned forward and placed her hands on the heartstone, the swirling in its depths casting light upon her face. She stared down at it, seemingly enraptured.

The song of the heartstone swelled, and Merry's gaze was once again pulled to it, her anger fading. She dug her nails into her palms, using the pain to ward off the magnetic draw it emitted. Her body throbbed with the need to touch it, to immerse herself in the song. She'd been mesmerised when she'd looked upon the Earth tree that was the physical embodiment of the Earth focal point. The Spirit focal point was in a cavern beneath the tower. It also called to her, but not the way the stone and its song did.

Her mind began to wander, losing itself in the song, and Merry dug her nails into her palms even harder. How was she going to keep blocking it? There had to be some way to shut it out. Maybe a different song would drown it out. She hummed a few bars of a song that never failed to get her to sing along, *Bohemian Rhapsody*, by Queen, and as the melody played out in her head, her attraction to the heartstone waned.

The moment the hum faded the attraction returned. She worked to keep the hum going in her head as she faced Ophelia. 'If you don't want to listen to what I have to say, then you might as well lock me back in my room. I will never swear an oath to the guild.'

Ophelia's head snapped up. 'I am not done with you yet. You leave when I say you can. First, you will tell my enforcers where Donna Syphera and Debra Mallory are hiding. They are fugitives and must be returned to the tower to begin their rehabilitation.'

Rehabilitation that was sure to include the swearing of the same oath she wanted Merry to swear. 'I'm not telling you anything.' Besides, she had nothing to tell. She had no idea where either mage was.

'Then perhaps I should see if starvation improves

your receptiveness, if you think it works so well for Lord Andel,' said Ophelia with a smirk.

Disgusted, Merry turned away. There was no reasoning with the mage leader. 'Starve me. Lock me up. Do whatever you want. I will not give in.' No, she would find a way to escape. She would get out of the tower, get her last two charms, make the transportation spell and get the hell out of Tirana.

Somehow.

Ophelia was clearly besotted or bewitched by the heartstone. Merry looked over at Gabriel and saw he was staring in horror at his aunt. After his previous attempts to convince Merry that she would do the right thing, it had to be a crushing blow to realise what she was capable of. As if he felt her gaze, he turned to look at her, and determination replaced the horror in his grey eyes. Like her, she knew he was ready to do whatever it took to ensure they escaped. The fate of Tirana depended on them. If they left it up to the guild, under Ophelia's rule, then they were all doomed.

Ophelia ranted and raved for ten more minutes, but Merry refused to respond to any of her barbed remarks or threats. Her mind was filled with plans to escape. The Spirit mage who was guarding her was staring at Ophelia, mouth agape, no longer muttering the spell to smother Merry's magic. Taking advantage of her guard's distraction, Merry carefully reached out with her Earth senses to decipher the layout of the tower.

The floor where she was being housed stood out as a

dead zone, devoid of almost all magic. There were small yet vibrant sparks of magic at four points around the edge of the circular tower, sparks that sang to her.

Heartstones, with streams of magic leading to the next one, created a chain around the inside of the tower. This had to be the warding spell, fused with the heartstones anchoring it in place. Merry gently touched her senses on one of the heartstones, changing the hum of her song to match the one it was singing. An unpleasant buzz rang through her head before she was mentally pushed away. A second and third attempt ended the same way, with the buzz becoming more painful each time.

The warding spell was deflecting her, and an attempt to dislodge the bricks around one of the heartstones proved just as unsuccessful. So, she couldn't destroy the ward from here. She pulled her senses back to observe the floor as a whole, seeking a crack in the ward, something, anything, that she could use.

One of the heartstones was at the edge of a stairwell narrower and steeper than the one she had been escorted down. This stairwell led down the side of the tower. It was at the opposite end of the hall to the one Merry had been brought down, nestled in the space between the outer wall and the first room.

Merry's room.

The heartstone anchor was set just behind a tiny spark of magic, and she was sure this was the compartment where her grandmother had hidden her journal and the amethyst. Unlike the anchor, this spark welcomed her mental touch. Once she figured out how to use it to escape her room, she could take the stairwell to the ground floor, and maybe detour to the Spirit focal point on the way. If she could get her Spirit charm now, she would never have to come back to this wretched tower.

When it became clear Merry was not listening and would not change her mind, a furious Ophelia ordered her to be taken back to her room.

Merry pulled her senses back just as her Spirit mage guard gave a start and spun around to glare at her, eyes narrowed with suspicion. Her lips once more moved as she voiced her silent spell. Eyes downcast, Merry tried to give the impression that she was not aware the mage had failed in her duty to keep her from accessing her magic. She was more than ready to escape to the quiet of her prison when Adrian indicated for her to move ahead of him. But before she left the grand hall she glanced at Gabriel. The handsome young mage took a step forward, and then grimaced as he was pulled up short by the enforcer holding his invisible leash.

'Gabriel,' said Ophelia, an ugly tone distorting her voice, 'explain to me, and the rest of the guild, how you let a pretty face get in the way of your duty.'

Merry winced at the words, and if not for Adrian's look of caution she would have turned around and blasted Ophelia. Anger kept her back straight as she was led from the hall and to the large space that appeared to have tripled in onlookers since she had been led through earlier. Merry smoothed down the front of her blue, green and white dress, studiously avoiding eye contact with any of the onlookers as the enforcers marched her through the crowd. But she could not avoid hearing the whispers.

Mostly it was her name. Well, hers or her grandmother's, though Gabriel was mentioned a lot as well, mainly in admiring tones by young women. Merry kept her head high until they reached the stairwell that led to her tower prison. The Spirit mage unlocked the door, and strode purposefully up the stairs, with Merry at her back and the enforcers close behind. The first three flights of stairs were easy to ascend, but Merry's legs started to ache as she headed up the fourth one, her breathing becoming laboured. She had lost so much physical condition thanks to winding up in a coma brought on by magical exhaustion and subsequently being locked away for a week with nothing to do but stress over her fate.

The Spirit mage showed no sign the climb affected her in any way, and Merry refused to ask for a rest. The sooner she was back in her prison room, the sooner she could start working on her escape. Still, she let out a relieved sigh when they reached the landing just below the prison level and she was ushered up the last few steps. A harsh whisper echoed in Merry's head as the Spirit mage unlocked the door and gestured for Merry to enter ahead of her.

Dead or alive, you will serve Lord Andel.

Merry faltered mid-step and was shoved hard in the back. She stumbled through the door and the familiar muffling returned as she lost access to her magical ability. She cast a backwards glance and saw the Spirit mage was now at her back, a bored expression on her thin face.

The threat had to have come from her. Only a Spirit mage would be able to contact her telepathically.

Before she could say anything, Adrian took her elbow and pulled her along with him to the door to her room. With his free hand he hurriedly unlocked it and then shoved her inside. As she turned around, he gave her a sharp nod, and then the door slammed shut between them, the sound of the lock engaging ringing in the silence.

Merry stared at the locked door for a long moment. Then she gave a shake and headed to the wing backed chair beside the fireplace. The fire was merrily blazing away, fresh firewood having been added while she was out, and her lunch tray was gone.

Despite the fire, Merry shivered, the threat lingering in her mind. She reached down and grabbed out her grandmother's journal, seeking to lose herself in the neatly scribed words, though she had already read them so many times she practically knew them by heart.

They were heartbreaking words, telling of a mother's anguish at being unable to return to her son.

The journal had not been a blueprint for escape as

Merry had initially hoped. Instead it detailed her grandmother's time in captivity, her fruitless quest to convince Ophelia that the direction she was taking the guild was the wrong one, along with regret that she had not been able to find her son's father and tell him about his child before she had been captured.

Sadie had told Merry she suspected her grandmother had been pregnant before she first travelled to the old world, and here was proof that would explain Merry's ability to use the heartstones Lord Andel's Earth witches had illegally mined for him.

Her true grandfather had been a Singer named Sylvester who had done the unthinkable and left his mountain home to forge a life in the open fields of Tirana. Her grandmother's journal said he felt he did not belong, a genetic mutation meaning he did not look like the rest of his brethren, a difference that was also reflected in his singing voice. Where the other Singers' voices were melodious and ethereal, his was a baritone that overpowered the songs of the others when they joined together.

He had stopped singing in the daily ceremony to imbue life and magic in the heartstones in the Cavern of Heart Songs, and then one day decided to leave. He had been young, handsome, his deep singing voice ensuring he always had a bed in any inn and plenty of admirers. Merry's grandmother had met him at one of those inns, while seeking the portal that would bring her to Belwich.

Clearly more than singing had taken place, as she was pregnant when she had crossed over. She had then met the man she would eventually fall in love with. He had helped her acclimatise to life in a more modern setting and claimed Merry's father as his own child, even going so far as to take the last name of Meadows to ensure the family name lived on.

Merry's grandfather, or the man she'd thought to have been her grandfather, had died before she was born, but her own parents had never said anything about him not being biologically related. Could it be her own father had never known the truth? And how had her grandmother explained where she had come from? All the journal said was that her grandmother never revealed the truth about Tirana, a fact she had come to regret the longer she was kept from returning to Belwich.

But as revealing as the journal was and as comforting as it was to know her grandmother had eventually been able to escape, the knowledge it had taken years ate away at Merry.

She didn't have years. She had weeks, maybe only days, before the witch hunters would be able to access the portal in her grandmother's bookshop and transport themselves to Tirana to continue their persecution of anyone who possessed magic. She had no time to sit around waiting for guild traitors to make good on the threat to have her serve Lord Andel.

She had to escape now.

Merry stood up and strode to the wardrobe that held her belongings. She shoved aside the clothes supplied by the guild then kneeled down as she reached for the strap that opened the little door that opened onto the gap in the wall, a gap her grandmother had painstakingly carved out during the decades she was imprisoned in this very room.

Merry reached a hand inside and concentrated on the feel of magic.

Ellen had said the gland that allowed witches and mages to do elemental magic was in their brain, and Merry's previous attempts to do any magic while she held her hand in the small compartment had failed. She'd thought the gland being in her head, which was too big to fit in the small compartment, was the reason it didn't work. But when she used her magic, it seemed to come from all over her body, and all around her, as she harnessed the elements of Air, Water and Earth. There had to be some way she could access the magic contained in this tiny spark.

The stairwell she had located while she was in the grand hall had to be on the other side of the wall, the small compartment reaching into it. If she could access enough of her Earth magic to break through into the stairwell and descend to the next level, she would have full use of her magic. The guild would not be able to prevent her from escaping then.

She'd need to find a way to find and free Gabriel as well but she was sure she would be able to do that. Then they could get away from crazy Ophelia and join up with Ellen, Sadie and Beethoven. She hadn't missed noting that Gabriel's familiar had not been at his side when they were in the hall and figured they were also being kept apart. Ophelia seemed to want them alone and demoralised, maybe thinking it would lead them to give up sooner.

Not happening. There was no way Merry was giving up. There was too much at stake.

She grabbed her staff and poked the end into the compartment. Running her hands over the swirls her magic had carved into it, she willed her Earth magic to waken. She envisioned it seeping through the rock behind the wardrobe, widening the cracks.

Nothing happened. All she got for her efforts was a pounding in her head.

She got to her feet and surveyed the wardrobe. It was solid timber, and her efforts to move it had not proved successful. But then, she had been taking care not to make it obvious that she wanted to get behind it, to further explore the magical compartment.

She was done with being careful. The telepathic threat had rung with the air of finality. She was not safe, locked in this tower room, just waiting for her enemies to spring whatever trap it was they were forming. But she could not act on her new plan until after the dinner meal had been delivered and she was less likely to be disturbed. Still, she could at least get prepared.

Merry pulled out all the clothes from the wardrobe,

stuffing the dresses the guild had supplied her with under the bed. Her dresses, the green one loaned to her by Ellen and the white one donated by a villager in Jeriton, she placed in her pack along with the rest of her belongings and set them on the floor of the small bathroom, refusing to contemplate the idea that this escape attempt would fail like all her others.

With her preparations done, she sat in the wing backed chair by the fire to wait, listening for the key in the lock, tensing when it finally came. She remained still and silent as four enforcers, one of them Branstone, escorted the servant with her dinner tray. The nervous servant darted many glances Merry's way, as if she expected to be attacked at any moment— not that Merry had done anything to her or any of the other servants who brought her meals— and placed the tray on the small table beside the chair. Merry's jaw was tense, as was the rest of her body, but she murmured a quiet 'thank you' the same as she did every time a meal was delivered. Then she waited for the enforcers and the servant to leave before moving.

She didn't eat. Her body was wound tight, her stomach churning at the thought of putting anything in it. Instead, she got up and grabbed the heavy poker from beside the fireplace before returning to the wardrobe. She first worked on the doors, using the poker to pry the hinges loose. Then she set to work dismantling as much of it as she could to make it as light as possible.

She refused to take a break even when her arms shook and sweat stung her eyes.

Magic might have been used to heal her from magical exhaustion, but her body was still not fully recovered. A week of sitting and doing nothing but stressing had robbed her of the physical strength she had gained from marching all over Tirana. Eventually she had as much of the wardrobe dismantled as possible and stood back to survey her work. Would it be enough? The wardrobe was built of solid timber, and her efforts to move it previously had not resulted in even a millimetre of movement.

But then, she was even more motivated now.

Merry moved to the side and forced the end of the poker into the slim gap between the back of the wardrobe and the rock wall of the chamber. She wedged it in as far as it would go and then worked to lever the wardrobe away from the wall. She strained every muscle she had, breath coming in gasps as she worked to move it. It did not budge. The plush carpet underfoot prevented it from sliding.

Merry stifled a curse as she dropped the poker and wriggled her fingers to ease the ache from holding it so tightly. Then she strode over to the bed and grabbed the coverlet. She tossed it on the floor and then pulled off the top sheet. It was a silky soft material. If she could wedge it under the front of the wardrobe maybe it would help it to slide.

She placed the sheet on the plush carpet in front of

the wardrobe and used the poker to push the ends under the edge as far as possible. Then she repositioned herself at the back of the wardrobe, hoping this time it would actually work. Pulse pounding in her head, Merry threw every scrap of energy she had left into moving the wardrobe, hands slick with sweat.

At first nothing happened. Then the wardrobe shifted. Only a millimetre or two, but it was more than she had ever achieved before. Hope flooding her with extra strength, Merry wedged the poker in further and readied herself to go again.

The sound of a key in the lock froze her breath.

No one came to her room after the evening meal was delivered.

Yet the door was opening, and Merry moved away from the wardrobe, gripping the poker tightly, as a tall figure in a hooded purple robe stepped into the room.

CHAPTER 3

*T*he newcomer stretched out her hands and Merry retreated, pressing her back against the wall beside the wardrobe. But the expected attack did not come. Instead, the mage folded back the hood of her robe and stared at Merry silently. This was not the thin faced Spirit mage from earlier, but a young woman, slender, with blond hair in intricate braids.

'Who are you? What do you want?' Merry widened her stance and raised the poker. Just because it was a different mage didn't mean this one wasn't also a member of Lord Andel's rebels.

'My name is Tara, and I need your help.' The young woman's voice was soft and filled with entreaty as she stepped farther into the room.

Merry snorted. 'In case you hadn't noticed, I'm a prisoner. No help to anybody.'

Tara's eyebrows raised and she waved a hand at the

wardrobe. 'From the looks of it, you don't intend on being a prisoner for long. But unless you know how to use magic in a warded room, there is no way you will be able to tunnel into the secret passage on the other side of that wall.'

Merry stiffened. 'I don't know what you're talking about. I was just redecorating.'

'We don't have time for this. I will help you escape, in return for your oath that you will rescue my mother. She is Britta Holmgren.'

'You're Britta's daughter?' Even as she spoke, Merry was mentally kicking herself for not realising it sooner. Tara looked much like her mother. She was missing Britta's air of leadership and hardness that had to have come from leading her group of rebel witches, but the same resoluteness was in her eyes.

Merry's shoulders slumped, the poker falling to the ground at her feet as she remembered her last sight of Britta, captured by Lord Andel's militia and being marched back to the manor house to be imprisoned in the dungeon and starved into submission.

She shook her head. 'I'm sorry, Tara. I wish I could help you, and your mother. But she's in Andelmine Province and I'm locked up here.'

'I know how to open the secret passage. I can help you escape. All you have to do is give me your oath.'

Tara clasped her hands in front of her chest, desperation on her face. 'Please, I don't want my mother to be enslaved by Lord Andel and made to use her magic to further his cause. The guild will not lift a finger to help her, or the other witches he has captured. I was in the great hall, and I heard what you said to Ophelia Fairweather. You know they need to be freed, and I'm offering you the chance to do it.'

Merry narrowed her eyes. Much as she longed to be free of the tower, she wasn't about to trust a complete stranger, no matter how impassioned her plea appeared to be. 'How did you even get in here? This floor is supposed to be guarded by enforcers.'

Tara flushed, hands once again falling to her sides. 'I tricked them, got them to come to the floor below and used my magic to put them to sleep.'

'Really?' Merry didn't bother hiding her scepticism. 'You're a guild mage, sworn to uphold guild law. Unless of course, you're one of the mages working for Lord Andel.' It was small comfort to know that like Merry, Tara would be unable to use magic on the prison floor. Just because she didn't appear to be armed didn't mean the other woman didn't possess a weapon of some kind. She could be hiding anything under her robe.

The colour bleached from Tara's face, and she shook her head. 'I would never willingly work for that man. He is a monster. He is torturing my mother and all those other witches. You said he is starving them into submission. Making them work for him against their will. My mother doesn't deserve any of that. She is a good person. All she ever wanted to do is take care of us, and to make sure witches got a fair go. She...' Tara's voice faltered, tears streaming down her cheeks.

Then she took a deep breath and stepped closer to Merry. 'Please, Miss Meadows, you have to help her. You were there. You know what it was like, what Lord Andel will be doing to her. You can't not care.'

Guilt at not doing more to help Britta and the others swirled in Merry's stomach. But she forced it down. She could not let emotion drive her actions. 'That still doesn't answer my question. How is it that you could go against your oath and use your magic to put the guards to sleep?'

'My training is complete, but I have not taken my final oath. I am still classed as an apprentice and will take my final oath at the next equinox, alongside those who have also competed their studies. Only then will I be considered a full mage.' Tara waved a hand down her front. 'I stole this robe from my mentor's room, to trick the guards into obeying my orders to descend to the floor below.'

Merry considered her for a moment, unable to tell if Tara was telling the truth or not. 'How do you know there is a secret passage behind this wall?' Since Tara had brought it up, there was no point hiding that she knew it was there.

'I am strongest in Spirit, but I also have a minor ability with Earth. Not strong enough to be classed as a mage, but enough to discern the space.'

It all sounded plausible, but Merry still hesitated to

trust Tara. The guild had gone to a lot of trouble to ward this entire floor against magic, to imprison all sorts of mages. They wouldn't make it easy for anyone to discover there was a hidden way, one that allowed magic, or people would have used it to free those captured. Her grandmother had never mentioned the stairwell in her journal, and she'd had mastery of all five elements.

Merry had only been able to find the wards, and what they concealed, because of the heartstones used as anchors for the spell that blocked all magic on the prison floor. Without her Singer heritage, she would be as blind as everyone else.

No, she couldn't trust Tara. Something wasn't right with her story. This had to be a trick.

As if she could sense where Merry's thoughts were headed, Tara pushed her shoulders back, chin raised, and a militant look in her eyes. 'If you don't agree to help me, I will summon the guards and they will make sure you never have a chance to escape.'

Merry bent down and scooped up the poker. 'You can't summon anyone if you're unconscious.' Tara had the key to her room. All Merry had to do was take it from her and she would be free. Once she found out which room Gabriel was locked away in, the two of them could figure out how to get into the secret passage.

Tara's tough stance deflated. 'I'm sorry for threatening to turn you in, but the spell I used to put the guards to sleep will not last much longer. If they find me here, I'll end up imprisoned in the room next to yours. We need to leave now, to have any hope of escaping and saving my mother. She is all I care about.'

Merry's heart panged at the desperation in Tara's voice. Was she wrong in thinking this was some kind of trick? Was her best opportunity for escape about to slip away?

Tara took another step closer, entreaty in her gaze. 'If you agree to help me, I can take you to the Spirit focal point. You need to collect a charm from it, yes?'

Merry's fingers clenched on the poker as she moved towards Tara, ready to strike. 'How do you know that?'

Tara backed up, panic in her voice as she said, 'The mages have been discussing your arrival in Tirana for many weeks. A witch of the Meadows bloodline is big news. I doubt there is any mage in Tirana who is not aware of you and your quest. All of us apprentices have been listening to the stories. Mage Fairweather may insist it was her guild mages who saved Marshland Province, but many here know she is hiding the truth from us. My friend's mentor was one of the Water mages who was there. She told us you saved her life, all of their lives, and nearly lost your own because of it. Magical exhaustion was the only reason the guild were able to capture you.'

Merry grimaced. Tara's words were true. She would never have come to the tower willingly.

'Enough of this,' said Tara. 'We are wasting time my mother does not have to spare. Will you swear an oath to save her, or will you remain a prisoner of the guild for the rest of your life?'

When she put it like that, Merry knew there was no real choice. She had to get out of the tower, and it would be easier to accomplish that with Tara's help. Not that she was going to trust her until she had proved herself. She would be ready to act if this turned out to be some kind of trap. 'All right, I'll do it.'

Relief flooded Tara's face. 'You have a heartstone. It's one of the charms for the spell to return you to your world. Hold it in your hands and make your oath.'

Merry stilled at the thought of swearing an oath on her heartstone. Would that make it binding, even though the floor was warded against magic?

Tara must have seen her hesitation, because she said, 'The oath will be as binding as you make it.'

Merry fetched her belongings from the bathroom and grabbed out her heartstone. It weighed heavily in her hand, reminding her of the devastation she had wrought with it when connected to the Earth focal point. Without the magical hum that usually accompanied it the burden was not so heavy.

She made a fist around the heartstone and faced Tara. 'I swear to do my best to free your mother and the other captured witches.'

Then she waited for Tara to protest that doing her best was not good enough, but all the other woman did was nod and then head for the door.

'We need to hurry. As I said, my spell will be wearing off soon.'

Merry tucked her heartstone into the pocket of her dress and then hefted her pack over one shoulder. Last, she scooped up her staff, ready to clobber Tara with it if necessary. When she had everything she wanted to take ready, she strode after the young mage.

As she exited her room, Merry peered down the hall to confirm it was empty of enforcers or other threats. Tara moved ahead of her, hurrying to the corner where Merry's room met the wall, hand up to probe the bricks.

'We need to get Gabriel Fairweather,' said Merry, scanning the closed doors nearest to her room. She had no idea which one was his room.

'There's no time,' said Tara, still pushing bricks in what appeared to be a set sequence. A low grating noise came as a section of the wall slid sideways, creating a narrow doorway. Then she beckoned for Merry to enter the shadowy gap ahead of her.

Merry didn't move. 'I'm not leaving without him.'

'He's Mage Fairweather's nephew. We can't trust him.'

'I trust him far more than I do you.' Merry shook her head. 'Do you have the keys to all the rooms?'

Tara gave a sigh, and then reached in to an inner pocket of her robe and produced a large brass key. 'This key opens all the doors, but I don't know what room he is in.'

'Then we try them all.' Merry stepped forward and

plucked the key from Tara's hand, and then proceeded to unlock and open the door across from her room. It was empty. So were the next two she tried. The fourth door opened, and she smiled at the sight of Gabriel sitting in a wing backed chair exactly the same as the one in her room. He appeared to be dozing, but he jumped to his feet the second she crossed the threshold, pleasure and surprise on his face.

'Merry.' He rushed over and hugged her.

It felt so good to be in his arms, to feel his hard body pressed up against hers as his familiar scent wrapped around her. She hugged him back for a moment, and then reluctantly pulled free of his embrace.

'We're leaving. Now,' she said.

He took a step back, his gaze roving over her and then flicking to the open doorway behind her. Merry glanced over her shoulder and saw Tara standing there, hands clasped in front of her chest.

'This is Tara Holmgren, the daughter of one of the witches Lord Andel has captured. I've sworn an oath to free her mother, in return for helping us escape.' No need to tell Gabriel that freeing him had not been part of Tara's plan.

Gabriel gave a nod and then strode quickly around the room, grabbing a few items out of his wardrobe and stuffing them into a pack similar to the one Merry carried before returning to her side.

'Let's go.'

Tara led the way back to the secret passage, which

opened onto a narrow set of stairs coated in darkness. 'I need to go last, to close the door, so it will take them longer to figure out how you escaped,' she said.

Merry wasn't sure she liked the idea of Tara being behind her, or of being the first one to enter the dark stairwell. It was impossible to see farther than the first landing with only the lights in the hall to illuminate the way. Gabriel showed no hesitation. He strode down the first few stairs and Merry quickly followed. There was a low grating sound behind her and then she was plunged into darkness when the door closed and sealed them within the stairwell.

Merry froze, heart pounding until she heard the soft movements of Tara behind her. Taking deep breaths, Merry reached out and placed a hand on the wall beside her, using it to steady herself as she moved down several more stairs. She was grateful when the muffling in her head lifted and she was able to command her staff to light up, banishing the immediate shadows and allowing her to see Gabriel ahead of her.

Sadie, can you hear me? Merry stretched out her senses, sending her mental call as far as she could.

Merry, thank goodness. I was worried when I connected with you earlier only to have the connection severed. My head has only just stopped aching from the backlash.

A Spirit mage was guarding me, stopping me from accessing my magic and talking to you. I'm free now. So is Gabriel. We're using a secret passage to get out of the tower.

I'm going to get my Spirit charm from the focal point below the tower, and then we will meet up with you and Ellen.

Beethoven tells me he is in contact with Gabriel. He says you are not alone.

Britta's daughter, Tara, is with us. She is the one who got us out and showed us the secret passage.

Do you trust her?

No, but I needed her help to escape. As quickly as possible, Merry explained about the oath she had made.

With the entire floor you were held on warded against magic, the oath will not have been a binding one even if it was made on a heartstone. But I sense this does not matter to you.

I should have done more to help Britta.

If you had, we would surely have been captured, and you would not have your Earth or Water charms, and Marshland Province would still be poisoned.

You don't know that. They had travelled down several floors while Merry was discussing this with Sadie, silence enveloping them. But now a new sound emerged from behind her.

Tara was crying. The sound was muffled, but it was unmistakable, and they weren't tears of joy that they were embarking on her plan to free her mother. Instinct had Merry stop and raise her staff as she twisted around to face Tara, ready to strike.

She was too slow. A wave of goosebumps swept over her, and a nightmarish vision burst into her head, freezing her in place.

Mage Fowler stood on the step above her, face

contorted in an expression of hate as his skeletal hands reached for her. Merry tried to scream but no sound came out, her vocal cords paralysed as she waited for the dead Spirit mage to burst her brains.

She wanted to shout at him, to tell him he was dead, that this couldn't be real, but fear had control of her, drowning out the tiny voice of reason. As the wave of goosebumps intensified Mage Fowler loomed over her, impossibly large as she cowered on the step below him.

There is no one to save you this time. No Earth tree to call on. I'm going to seal you up in the earth and you will live in endless torment right beside me.

Dimly, Merry heard Gabriel shouting something about a spell, and she tried to tear her eyes away from the vision of Fowler, to pull her mind from the brink. She dropped her staff to grasp her head in both hands, plunging the stairwell in darkness as she covered her eyes, desperate to block out the nightmare. But it was no use. She could still see him.

A loud crack sounded in Merry's head, and she was no longer standing in the stairwell. She was back at the Earth focal point, the crack in the ground that had swallowed Fowler now gaping open and his dead body hovering in the air above it. Blood dripped from the torn flesh in his nightmarish face as he gave a cruel laugh and gestured towards her.

There was a tug on her body, and she was propelled forward, suspended in the air above the chasm alongside Fowler. Then they both descended into the earth. As it began to close over them, he wrapped skeletal arms around her, his ruined flesh dripping blood and coating her with it. She couldn't breathe, pain engulfing her body as jagged rocks cut into her flesh. The sides of the chasm pressed against her, crushing her. Awareness flared in her head. She was going to die yet remain trapped forever in a nightmare where Fowler tortured her over and over again.

She heard someone cry out in pain and the vision vanished as quickly as it had appeared. Merry was back in the stairwell, huddled against the wall, body shuddering, sure she could still feel the earth closing around her, suffocating her. She forced her muscles to move, hunting for her staff in the darkness, hands shaking as she lifted it up and commanded it to light.

In the sudden glow, she spotted Gabriel crouched several steps below her, looking just as shaken as she felt. Then she turned to look behind her, leaning against the wall of the stairwell with legs that felt like they were going to collapse at any moment. Tara stood rigid, with her jaw clenched as she fought invisible bonds. Behind her stood Adrian, the enforcer's face a mask of determination as he extended a clenched fist towards the young Spirit mage.

'It was a nightmare spell,' said Gabriel, his voice hoarse as he slowly scaled the steps and reached Merry's side. 'Are you all right?' He put a hand on her shoulder.

Merry shook her head, struggling to dispel what she

had seen, to convince her body and mind that none of it had been real.

A nightmare spell was what Donna Syphera had used against the militia guarding the witches imprisoned in Greystone. No wonder they had been unable to do anything except scream and cower under their desks, if that was the kind of thing the spell made you see. She fought down bile as the image of the reanimated version of Fowler hung in her mind. Resolutely, she pushed it aside and focused on Tara. Her cheeks were still wet from her tears, and she must have realised Adrian was not about to release her for her shoulders had slumped.

Gabriel pushed away from the wall and nodded at Adrian. 'Thank you, my friend.'

'Don't thank me,' said Adrian, voice as hoarse as Gabriel's had been moments before. 'I am bound by my oath to do whatever is necessary to uphold guild law. I cannot let you escape. I must do everything within my power to detain you until reinforcements arrive.' Despite his words, the enforcer made no move to use his telekinetic ability to immobilise either Merry or Gabriel, and she knew he was capable of subduing more than one person at a time.

Gabriel would have realised this also, as he simply inclined his head. 'My thanks remain heartfelt. If not for your timely intervention, Merry and I would have been at the mercy of this young lady and her nightmare spell.'

'I'm sorry. I had no choice.' Tara's voice was weak, defeated.

'There is always a choice,' said Gabriel, his voice kind and calm. 'What I do not understand is why you would bother to free us if you only planned to attack us.'

'That wasn't the plan. I was supposed to lead Merry into a trap, at the Spirit focal point. But when I realised she knew something was wrong, I panicked.' Her eyes gleamed with fresh tears as she stared at Merry. 'I didn't want to hurt you, but the man said my mother would suffer if I didn't help them. He said he could guarantee she would not be hurt or enslaved by Lord Andel if I did what he wanted.

Merry grimaced. 'I knew I couldn't trust you.'

'All I care about is saving my mother. I didn't want to do this. I had no choice.'

'Mage Holmgren, your oath to the guild should have prevented you from using a nightmare spell against us,' said Gabriel quietly. 'Or did you find a way around taking it.'

Air hissed through Merry's teeth. Tara had lied about not being a fully-fledged mage, and Gabriel thought she was like Karl Piermont, recruited by Lord Andel's renegade mages. Was everything Tara told her a lie?

Tara went to shake her head but was still immobilised by Adrian. She winced, and then said, 'I took the oath, but the man who approached me used a heartstone to break it, and a second to bind my oath to obey him. Then he showed me another heartstone, one he said would be used to force my mother to obey Lord Andel. He had a whole bag of them, enough to enslave hundreds of witches and mages, and he can make the oath binding even if they refuse to speak it, as he did to me.'

Merry gasped. That was impossible. Hadn't she stopped Lord Andel mining more heartstones?

'Who is this man? Is he a Spirit mage?' Was a man like Fowler waiting to spring his trap on her?

'He's not a mage. He's something different. I've never seen anyone like him.' Tara shuddered, and then she broke down in sobs. 'I've failed him, and he's going to make my mother pay.'

'Merry?'

Gabriel's quiet voice pulled Merry's thoughts. She turned to face him.

'What are you going to do now?'

Merry stared at him, thoughts racing through her mind. A few moments ago everything had seemed simple. Get her Spirit charm, flee the tower and reconnect with her friends, save Britta and the other witches.

Tara's betrayal changed everything.

CHAPTER 4

There was no hint in Gabriel's face of what he thought Merry should do. This was her decision. She looked over to Adrian next, but all the reaction he gave her was a grimace and a gruff command to hurry and make up her mind. Finally she faced Tara, taking in the tears still trickling down her cheeks.

Merry took a deep breath. 'My oath may not be binding, but someone needs to rescue Britta and the others. If the guild won't do it, then it is up to us.'

'You'll still save her, even after I betrayed you?' Hope warred with caution in Tara's gaze.

'This isn't about you. It's about doing the right thing. No one should be forced to submit to someone like Andel.' Merry didn't add that she felt guilty about not doing more to help Britta when she was first captured. Sadie might say she'd had no choice, but the guilt roiling in her gut said otherwise. She straightened her shoulders and eyed Tara.

'I can't promise anything, but I will do my best to free your mother and the others.'

Fresh tears spilled down Tara's cheeks. 'Thank you. Thank you so much. Please, let me come with you. I want to help. I want to see my mother.'

Merry shook her head. 'You're oath bound to Lord Andel. Until that is broken, I can't trust you.'

The young Spirit mage shook her head. 'I'll fight it. I'll do whatever it takes. Please, let me join you. If you don't, I will follow you anyway. It's my mother.'

Gabriel stepped closer. 'What were the terms of the oath Andel's man bound you with?'

Tara hesitated with her eyes downcast. Then she took a deep breath and looked Gabriel squarely in the eye. 'To obey any direct order given by him, Lord Andel or his lieutenant, Karl Piermont.'

Merry stiffened. 'Karl was here?'

Tara shook her head. 'No. It was a black-haired man with the heartstones who bound my oath.' She frowned. 'I thought he was a Spirit mage, at first, as we have all been told they are the only ones who can bind an oath, but I did not sense any magic from him. Instead, he sang a strange song. I felt it reverberate throughout my entire body, connecting me to the heartstone, forcing me to accept the oath. Once he finished, he ordered me to unleash a nightmare spell on some of the men accompanying him, and I had to obey. The oath gave me no choice.'

'So if you were with us, while we rescued your mother, and this man, Lord Andel or Karl Piermont ordered you to attack us you would have to do it, no matter how much you tried to fight it.' Gabriel's voice was gentle. 'They could order you to attack your mother, and you would have no choice but to obey. Could you live with the consequences if that were to happen?'

Tara's hopeful expression crumpled into despair, and Merry was sure the only reason she was still upright was because of the invisible bonds Adrian had wrapped around her. After a long moment, she regained her composure and gave a slow nod. 'I understand. I will not try to follow you, not if it would endanger my mother.'

Adrian frowned down at her. 'You won't get a chance. You are a traitor to the guild. You will be locked up in a warded room until such time as Mage Fairweather has decided your punishment.'

Merry winced at the thought of Tara being subjected to the fate she had just escaped from. But she hadn't been wrong in saying they couldn't trust her. She had tried to lead Merry into a trap. Speaking of which…

'What were your orders regarding me?'

Tara grimaced. 'I was to convince you to trust me, and then lead you to the Spirit focal point so they can capture you. He has five mages with him, one for each element, all of them loyal to Lord Andel. He has soldiers with him too, at least a dozen.' She shot a sideways glance at Adrian. 'I feel the compulsion to lead you into his trap even now. If not for Master Irvine's ability making it impossible for me to move, I would still be trying to get you there. The longer we stand here the more uncomfortable it makes me feel. Every inch of my body is screaming at me to obey.'

Merry winced, remembering a similar feeling when she had wanted to run across the great hall and grab hold of the heartstone on the dais. It had been Adrian's telekinetic ability that had stopped her from making a colossal mistake until she had been able to use her hum to block out the call. But Tara didn't have any Singer blood to help her out of this predicament. Even as Merry watched, the young mage's features contorted with pain. They had to do something, to spare her from going through this.

Before she could say a word, Adrian raised his free hand and clenched his fist. Panic filled Tara's eyes, her mouth open and gasping for air. Merry lunged forward, to help her, only to have Gabriel grab her arm and hold her back.

'It's for the best,' he said, though his tone was bleak. 'Adrian will not hurt her, and we can't afford for her to hear our plans.'

Tara's eyes rolled back in her head, her body limp as the enforcer lowered her to the stairs. Gabriel let go of Merry's arm and she kneeled beside the young mage to check that she was breathing. While she might understand the reasoning behind suffocating Tara until she was unconscious, that didn't mean she was happy about it.

Gabriel bent over and fished in Tara's inner pocket for the brass key that had unlocked their doors. He straightened up and held the key out to the enforcer. 'Adrian, you need to take Tara back to the prison floor. Lock her in one of the rooms. It will not cancel out her oath, but it will help to dull the pain of failing to obey.'

Adrian grimaced. 'I need to lock all three of you up. My own oath is chafing.' Sweat beaded his brow and his hands were fisted. 'You are all deemed traitors to the guild. I can't allow you to escape.'

Despite his words, Adrian did not move even though it appeared he was in as bad a state as Tara had been before she had been rendered unconscious.

Gabriel surveyed his friend calmly. 'What does your oath consider the more important course of action? Recapture two escaped prisoners you know pose no threat to the guild, or apprehend those that seek to overthrow it?'

Adrian stiffened, and his eyes narrowed. 'What do you suggest?'

'According to Tara, Lord Andel's supporters have infiltrated the tower. My aunt decreed that any mage who supports him is a traitor not just to the guild but to all of Tirana. Apprehending these mages should be of the utmost priority, don't you agree?'

Calm settled over the enforcer, a wry grin curving

his lips. 'Indeed.' He hefted Tara into his arms and gave Gabriel a nod. 'I will lock this one up and join my brethren. I will have to immediately report your escape as well as the incursion.'

'I understand,' said Gabriel. 'Thank you, my friend.'

Adrian shifted to look at Merry. 'Tell Miss Hayland I'm sorry.' Then he turned and strode back up the stairs, moving fast despite the burden he carried.

Gabriel touched Merry on the arm, drawing her attention back to him. 'We need to go, now. Adrian will not be able to buy us much time.'

Merry gripped her belongings and hurried down the stairs. She had never liked the enforcer, but she had to respect his actions, even if he would be compelled to sound the alarm for their escape as soon as he could. They were lucky the need for him to apprehend the people waiting to capture her took precedence.

As she hurried down the stairs as fast as was safe, she sent out her senses. The Spirit focal point called to her, and she wished there was some way to get to it and find her charm. She could sense a large group of people waiting there. Most of them were a dull light, indicating they were not magic users, and had to be the soldiers Tara had mentioned. Five others flared with the colour of their elemental ability, the mages. But there was one that flared with a blue and purple hue, shot through with silver. Not the purple of Spirit or blue of Water. This reminded her of the swirling colours that lit up her heartstone.

This had to be the man Tara said had been able to bind her oath without needing her acceptance.

As she focused on the stranger's aura, it pulsed stronger and she felt a deep pull inside her body, the urge to go to him. She and Gabriel had reached the bottom floor, and he headed down a corridor to the left, but Merry's steps faltered, that pull tugging her to the right.

Gabriel must have sensed she was not right behind him because he stopped and clasped her hand. 'Merry, there is no time for you to get your Spirit charm, even if we could avoid Andel's men. Adrian will have told the first enforcer he sees that we have escaped. His oath will allow him to do no less.'

Merry shook her head. 'It's not that. It's...' How could she explain the draw she felt? It was similar to what she had experienced when she had looked at the immense heartstone back in the grand hall. Yet it emanated from the flickering fire that represented the person with the heartstones. As Merry focused, she could even sense the heartstones he held, their song a soft lament inside her head.

The song strengthened the longer she listened to it, urging her forward. Gabriel tugged on her hand, but Merry ignored him, instead focused on the song. She pulled her hand free and made to step down the hall that would eventually lead her to the Spirit focal point.

A shrill alarm rent the air, drowning out the song in her head. Merry gasped in air and shook her head, shaking off the lingering beats of the siren song. She didn't resist as Gabriel grabbed her hand and pulled her towards the left corridor. They picked up speed as they went, the alarm making conversation impossible. They rounded a corner and found themselves in a small stone alcove, a wooden door, barred and locked, blocking their passage.

Merry could sense grass and trees beyond the door.

This was the way out.

She summoned her elemental ability as she clasped the lock and it crumpled in her hand. Gabriel lifted the heavy strip of wood and tossed it aside as Merry pushed the door open. After days of being inside a room with no windows, the fresh scents on the air were a heady perfume as Merry rushed outside into the chill night. Gabriel followed and slammed the door shut behind him.

'There is nothing to bar the door on this side,' he said.

Merry stepped up and placed a hand on the stones to the side of the door, willing them to bend around the hinges and the cracks at the edges, sealing the door. 'That will hold until they find an Earth mage to release the door,' she said as she hefted her staff and eyed Gabriel.

'We need to be long gone by then.' He lifted his pack and they set off.

Sadie was a welcome presence in Merry's head, and she guessed Beethoven was the same for Gabriel as they both headed in the same direction. Merry let the little black familiar guide her steps as they hurried through the copse of trees that butted up against the side of the tower. The grass underfoot was thick and lush, and numerous bushes tugged and caught at her skirt as she hurried through. There was no time to use her Earth magic to ease their passing, and it would be a beacon to other Earth users if she did so.

Sadie and the others waited not far from the tower, hidden in a low valley, but to get to them Merry and Gabriel would have to crest a hill denuded of trees or any other form of cover, meaning they would be visible to anyone looking their way from the tower.

The alarm was abruptly silenced behind them, but Merry did not take it as a good sign. She burst out of the cover of the trees and made for the base of the hill, with Gabriel easily keeping pace at her side. She was sure he could go faster, but was matching his speed to hers, the week of being cooped up not adversely affecting his fitness.

There was no time to be disgruntled about not being as fit or as fast as him. Shouts rose behind them, the outcry signalling they had been spotted. As she reached the base of the hill, Merry chanced a glance behind her and saw a group of enforcers breaking through the trees. But their attention was not focused on her and her companion.

Instead they were running across the clearing,

towards another hill, to where a large party of people were grouped around five figures in mage robes.

That had to be Lord Andel's men.

Even as she had the thought, the Air mage called on the wind and the first row of enforcers reeled backwards as a huge gust struck them. Goosebumps raced over Merry's arms as the other mages in the group threw their own magic into the fray. The ground rumbled beneath her feet, while fire flashed through the air. They had to get out of there before the mages finished with the enforcers and targeted her and Gabriel.

Lungs laboured, legs aching. Merry raced up the hill alongside Gabriel. At the top, she stopped to gather her breath, gaping at the battle that took place on the other hill. More enforcers and mages streamed out from the tower to join the fight. But it was the sight of a man standing slightly apart from Lord Andel's people that caught Merry's attention.

He was tall, black hair streaked with silver, his aura blazing with the purple and blue of heartstones. She could not see his features clearly, yet she knew he was looking at her, and the song from before thrummed through her body. This time it did not urge her to come to him. Instead it prickled at her skin, seeking to chase her away.

A shout came from nearby, and Merry whirled to see that a smaller group of enforcers and mages from the tower was coming their way.

'We need to go,' said Gabriel.

Merry turned back to look at the other hill. The black-haired man was no longer in sight and his forces were retreating, mages and enforcers in pursuit. The prickling against her skin did not let up and Merry heeded its warning as she ran as fast as she could down the other side of the hill. They reached a set of trees near the base and Merry reached out to grab Gabriel's hand, pulling him to a stop.

She recited her invisibility spell in her head as the first enforcer appeared at the top of the hill and looked in their direction. Pressure built in her head as more people joined him, all of them scanning for her and Gabriel. None of them saw them.

As her racing heart slowly settled, Merry watched as the group from the tower continued to search, never letting her litany cease.

It seemed to take forever, but finally their pursuers moved away and Merry took her first easy breath in a long time. She and Gabriel remained where they were, not moving until Merry could no longer sense anyone nearby. Her muscles were stiff and sore from staying in the same position for so long, and her head ached from maintaining the invisibility spell. But if she was able to sense the whereabouts of people nearby then so could the Earth mages bound to the guild.

The thought that other mages might be able to make an invisibility spell to cloak themselves and others worried at her as she and Gabriel made their way to where Ellen and the familiars were camped. Donna Syphera had been surprised by how strong Merry's invisibility spell had been, and she supposed mages with all five magical elements were rare, but that didn't mean there weren't others out there.

But there was no sign anyone followed them.

Dawn was approaching when they finally made their way to the camp. Sadie was waiting for Merry at the edge, ears perked, tail high and her yellow eyes bright.

Merry dropped to her knees, shucked off her pack, and scooped the little cat into her arms. 'I am so glad to see you.' She burrowed her face into the soft fur, breathing in the fresh scent that was uniquely cat.

Sadie melted in her arms, a purr rumbling through her tiny body even as her tart voice sounded in Merry's head. *Just because I'm letting you cuddle me as if I were a common house cat does not mean I will tolerate similar displays in future. I realise that you have undergone a traumatic ordeal, but I do have the dignity of a companion to uphold.*

Merry smiled as she gently placed the little cat on the ground. *I would expect nothing less from such a dignified companion, and I appreciate you allowing me to take these liberties, in light of my traumatic ordeal.*

With a pleased sniff, Sadie stretched forward and gently bit down on Merry's left wrist, her sharp teeth not breaking the skin. *I am glad to have you returned to us. It has been lonely in my head, with only Beethoven to talk to.*

Merry looked over to where Beethoven was not

showing any sign he found being cuddled in Gabriel's arms to be undignified.

Sadie's next sniff was haughty. *Of course not! He is a mere familiar, after all.*

Beethoven's head swivelled and he fixed his light green eyes on Sadie. *Familiar or companion, the words mean the same thing, and I know you are just as pleased by the safe return of our charges as I am.* He lifted his gaze to Merry. *I thank you for your insistence that Gabriel be part of the rescue. Otherwise, I fear he would remain as a prisoner of his aunt for some time.*

Merry stiffened at the reminder of the leader of the mage guild. She got to her feet and faced Gabriel. 'Your aunt is under the spell of that heartstone.' She described what she had observed and how the heartstone had called to her as well.

'I was afraid of that. She was acting unlike herself.' He was silent a moment. 'Is it wrong that I am glad it is a stone that has caused her to behave so erratically? After the deaths of my parents, thanks to a rogue mage, she was the backbone of our family. I would not be where I am today if it was not for her.'

Merry shook her head. 'That's not wrong at all. She's family.' Her heart ached at the thought of her own parents. She had not always understood their restrictions on what books she could read or television shows or movies she could watch as she grew up, and she'd railed against their idea of what was appropriate for a girl her age to do, but she never doubted that they loved her.

Understanding now, how her father's behaviour had been shaped by the disappearance of his mother, Merry's grandmother, and how her re-emergence in his life and talk of magic had helped to form his code of ethics, she knew he would be devastated by her own disappearance. She had to find a way back to her world, to show him her grandmother's journal and how it detailed a mother's grief at being separated from her son for so long. After decades of mystery and then distrust, her father might not be ready or willing to believe in the words it held but he deserved to know the truth. All of it.

The discussion that would reveal her grandmother had been pregnant before she had met the man Merry had grown up believing to be her grandfather was not one she looked forward to having. But that was in the future. For now, she had two more charms to collect before she could have a chance at getting home. With this new quest to free Britta, Gregor and the others, that possibility was even farther away as she followed Sadie to where Ellen was putting out the coals of a small fire pit.

Ellen brushed her hands against her emerald-green dress, a relieved smile on her face as she hurried to Merry and enveloped her in a warm hug. As with Sadie, Merry drank in the familiar scents of her friend, the herbs in the satchel that was always nearby.

'Thank the stars you are okay. I was so worried about you.' Ellen relaxed her hug enough to lean back and scan Merry's face. 'Are you well? No lingering effects from magically exhausting yourself?' Ellen's voice was filled with concern.

'I'm fine.' Merry hugged her friend once more and then stepped back. 'As good as new.'

'Are you sure? You were in a coma for days. I'm sure the guild healers know what they are doing, but magical exhaustion of that level is not something they would be accustomed to healing. What if they missed something?' A frown creased Ellen's brow as she reached up one hand to clutch her heartstone and rested the other on Merry's shoulder.

Ellen's lips moved in a silent spell as first goosebumps and then a wave of warmth rushed through Merry's body.

Merry stood patiently as she waited for her friend to assure herself that she was indeed completely healthy. As far as she could tell, now that she was well away from the warded tower, there was no change in either her health or her magical ability since before she went up against the poison stone at the Water focal point.

After a long moment, Ellen gave a relieved sigh. 'You really are well.' She gave Merry another quick hug and then stepped back, turning to Gabriel. 'I am also glad to see that you are well, Mage Fairweather.'

'Please, call me Gabriel. We are all fugitives from the guild. There is no need to be so formal.' He gave her a quick smile and then scanned the small campsite. 'You have been staying here for the past week?'

Ellen gave a quick nod. 'I knew Merry would find a way to escape, and I wanted to be close. Sadie and Beethoven seemed to be of the same mind.' She cast a fond smile towards the two familiars. 'They made it clear they were not budging until we were all reunited, and Sadie in particular has a way of making her opinions know.' She rubbed at one wrist.

'She bit you again? Sadie!' Merry shook her head reprovingly at the little black cat, who took no notice of the scolding as she groomed her sleek fur.

'Only once, a short time ago, and only to make me understand that you were on your way. Though I have no idea how you managed your escape.'

'There is no time for the tale now,' said Gabriel. 'Adrian had to report our escape and there are hunting parties searching for us. We need to go, now.'

'Adrian was with you?' Ellen's face fell. 'He was the one that sounded the alarm, wasn't he? Even here we could hear it.'

'He had no choice, though I know he would much rather have come with us.' Gabriel said kindly. 'He asked us to tell you he was sorry.'

Ellen gave a nod, eyes downcast as she packed up the remains of her camp and then they all set off into the dawn, ready to attempt the impossible once again.

CHAPTER 5

*I*f not for the threat of being discovered by the bands of enforcers and guild mages that were searching for them, and the urgency of their mission setting a breakneck pace, the trek through the woods would have been pleasant for Merry. She was out of the tower, able to breathe fresh air, and had been reunited with Sadie and Ellen. Having Gabriel and Beethoven with them made it even better. But this was not just a leisurely jaunt through the woods with friends. Lives were at stake.

Though they set a fast pace, warming her muscles, a chill wind reminded Merry that time was running out. It was not just for Britta and the others, though they had to reach Andelmine Province and rescue them before the black-haired stranger arrived with heartstones to enslave them. Merry also had her own deadline. She had to complete the rescue mission so she could then resume her quest to get her fire charm.

They had to stop numerous times before dawn began to lighten the sky, with Merry casting her invisibility spell anytime they encountered people. It wasn't just enforcers they had to look out for. The land they travelled through was more populated than the areas of Tirana Merry had ventured to so far, with farms that provided food to the town that wound around the lake on the other side of the guild tower. As well as farms, there were cottages for those who wished to live close to the guild tower but not right near it and also small villages dotting the landscape.

It wasn't that they had anything to fear from the farmers or villagers, but the fewer people to see them meant the fewer people who could pinpoint their direction for the guild.

Once they cleared inhabited land, they were able to travel faster, and with less chance of stumbling across passers-by, Merry was able to relax her vigilance. Her head pounded from maintaining her invisibility spell for so long, and she gratefully accepted Ellen's ministrations when they took a short break beneath a stone bridge.

'You shouldn't be pushing yourself so hard,' said Ellen, her touch gentle as she massaged Merry's temples.

Warmth rippled over Merry's scalp as the healer's magic soothed the worst of the ache.

'I'll be fine,' she said with a quick smile. 'I can't sense

anyone nearby, so I won't need to do any magic for a while.'

Gabriel stood at her side; his expression just as concerned as Ellen's. 'You won't do Britta any good if you push yourself to the verge of magical exhaustion again.'

'Britta?' Ellen's eyebrows rose. 'Is this the same Britta we met in Andelmine Province? The one Lord Andel's militia captured?'

Merry gave a weary nod. There hadn't been time since they met up to discuss her plan to free the captured witches with her friend. Even Sadie knew only some of it. With all Merry's concentration needed for the invisibility spell there had been little left over for telepathic communication.

'I'm going to rescue Britta and the others.' She briefly explained the encounter with Tara, ending with, 'I owe it to Britta to do everything I can to help them.'

'We owe her,' said Ellen firmly.

I know you feel great guilt at not being able to assist the rebels, but I fear we are running out of time to renew the wards around the portal.

Merry looked to Sadie. 'I know,' she said. 'But I have a plan that will help with that, I hope.' She shared Sadie's concern with Gabriel and Ellen, and then said. 'Britta and the others won't be able to stay in Andelmine once we rescue them. Lord Andel will do whatever it takes to capture them again. If we can get Britta to agree to stay at Dryton, they will be able to monitor the portal, to make sure no witch hunters get through.'

'The portal that brought you here is at Dryton?' Gabriel asked.

Merry nodded. 'It is close by. If I fail, if I cannot get the last two charms in time, I want you to tell your aunt where it is.' She took a deep breath, committing herself to this course of action. 'She can get guild mages to close it for good, to stop the witch hunters.'

'If the portal is closed, you will never be able to return to your world.' Ellen placed a hand on Merry's arm, concern in her gaze.

Merry worked hard to keep her voice light, to not show her fear at the thought of being trapped in Tirana for the rest of her life, as she said, 'The guild missed this portal. Maybe they missed others. Or I might find another way home. Who knows, I might become such a powerful mage that I could make my own portal.' She chanced a laugh, though it sounded brittle to her ears.

If there was another portal, one that had not been warded by your grandmother, the witch hunters would have found and used it by now. But if any witch or mage would be able to discover the means to make a new one I am sure it would be you.

Heartened by Sadie's faith in her, though she had only cast out the idea of making a new portal as a false hope, Merry continued, 'Either way, with Lord Andel willing to do whatever it takes to become King, Tirana is in greater threat from him than witch hunters at the moment. I'll never be able to get the Spirit charm if he gains control of the guild tower. Freeing Britta and the others will weaken him and help to make Tirana stronger if the witch hunters do manage to get through the portal.'

'You're right,' said Gabriel. 'I fear Tirana is on the brink of civil war. Once he has massed enough power, Andel will march on the guild tower. My aunt is wrong in thinking he could never be a threat, not if he has all the witches under his command, as well as rogue mages and ones like Tara who are forced to obey him. There is no telling how many more mages or those in training that have been forced to swear an oath by this new man of his.'

Merry shivered at the reminder of what they faced and from remembering the cold look in the eyes of the black-haired man as he'd stared at her from the hilltop back at the tower. There was no telling what would have happened if they hadn't been chased by enforcers.

He was out there somewhere, with his perverted heartstones. They had to get to Andel's manor and free Britta and the others before he got there.

Ellen delved into her pack and pulled out three waterskins, filling them from the stream running under the bridge. Then she dosed each waterskin with herbs and performed her spell to enhance their energy, before handing one each to Gabriel and Merry. The magically enhanced water tingled on her tongue as Merry sipped it, and then she placed some in her hand for Sadie to lap at. As she replaced the stopper, Merry indicated their break time was over. They would have to march on through the night and hope they could get ahead of Andel's men.

Now that her head was no longer pounding, Merry set her consciousness roving all around them, but felt no relief at only discovering the spark of animals. What if the black-haired man had already got past them? With Adrian and the rest of the enforcers on his tail, as well as guild mages, he should have found it hard to get away. Small hope that he and his companions had been captured and were now languishing in the guild tower's prison floor. He and his group of magic users had been able to infiltrate the tower unseen, and Gabriel was right in surmising Tara wouldn't have been the only one they had subverted. Merry was still sure the Spirit mage who had escorted her to the grand hall was a supporter of Andel's.

With the guild being undermined from within, by both willing and unwilling mages, they would have to operate under the assumption their enemy was still out there, also racing to get to Andelmine Province. Merry quickened her pace, though it was Gabriel who was in the lead as he was more familiar with the path they had to take. Ringed in mountains as Andelmine Province was, they were headed for a pass similar to the one she and Ellen had used when they made their way to the Earth focal point.

'It is not as well-known as the main pass,' Gabriel

assured her. 'I have no doubt Andel will have it guarded, but I am hoping it will be a small enough force that we will be able to use our magic to slip past them. It is closer than the main pass, also, so we will save time and come out nearer to Andel's manor than if we were to travel along the main road.'

Merry hoped he was right. With each step she took, her fear that they would be too late grew. She had to prevent Britta from being enslaved by Andel. If she was able to free her, Merry did not look forward to having to tell her that her daughter had been caught in the would-be king's web.

Hours passed, and Merry worked to ignore the grumbling in her stomach that made her regret not eating dinner before escaping the tower. Ellen's magic water was wearing off, leaving her tired and hungry, but she did not want to stop, as each step was bringing them closer to the pass and to freeing Britta and the other witches. Then she stumbled over a tree root, the light from her staff going out. It was Gabriel's quick reflexes that saved her from falling headfirst onto the ground.

'Enough,' he said, tone firm. 'You may think it fine to traipse about in the dark for hours on end, but I do not. It is past midnight. We need to stop and rest and eat. Once it is light we can continue, with less risk of breaking our necks in the dark.'

Merry gave a sigh as she commanded her staff to glow once more. He was right. Despite the timer she felt ticking down, they would be even slower if one of them seriously injured themselves. She scanned the trees nearby and realised her stumble had come at an opportune moment. They were on the verge of a small clearing, one just large enough for them to camp comfortably overnight. There was no conveniently placed stream to fill their waterskins, but it would do.

Ellen bustled into the centre of the clearing, setting up a fire pit which she had blazing within moments. Then she produced a small pot and poured a measure of water into it. She added thin slices of dried mushrooms and other vegetables, as well as herbs for seasoning. While the soup heated, Merry and Gabriel rolled out the bedrolls Ellen had prepared for them.

Once the soup was hot enough, Ellen added flour to thicken it and parcelled it out into three wooden mugs. Then she delved into her pack and pulled out round bread rolls that were surprisingly heavy given their small size.

'How did you know to have all this ready?' Merry waved the hand holding the bread roll at the pack of food and the bedrolls.

Ellen smiled as she blew on her mug to cool the soup. 'I've known you long enough now to know you would not reman a prisoner for long. I knew you would find a way out and wanted to be prepared.' She arched an eyebrow in Gabriel's direction. 'I was also sure you would not be alone. I was there when Mage Fairweather proclaimed that you would be locked in the tower after receiving your healing. Gabriel did everything he could to sway his aunt, to no avail, but he promised me he would do whatever it took to set you free.'

Merry looked over at Gabriel, flushing at the intent gaze he wore as he watched her.

He never took his eyes from her as he said, 'I hoped it would be my ability to negotiate that would win your freedom, and mine, but unfortunately my aunt was not to be swayed. But when I saw you in the grand hall, saw the look on your face when you realised she was spelled in some fashion, I knew the tower would not hold you much longer. Our subsequent escape came even quicker than I expected.'

With a snort, Merry said, 'Who knew it would be Lord Andel who came to my rescue. If he hadn't arranged for Tara to be subverted, we would probably still be locked in the tower. It would have taken forever for me to break through the wall between my room and the secret passage. It took my grandmother years to make even a small hole to access the magic pooled around the warding spell's anchor point.'

'What?'

Merry explained about the gap her grandmother had created to hide her journal and the amethyst, pulling them out to show them. 'She never doubted that she would one day get back to my world, no matter how many years passed, but the way the anchor was warded meant she could never use the magic to do much more than to buoy her spirits.'

'How did she escape then?' Ellen asked.

'I don't know,' said Merry. 'The journal stops mid-entry.'

'Like us, she had help. After her escape, an investigation revealed the servant who carried her meals also carried notes to those who supported Mage Meadows and others like her,' said Gabriel. 'They created a commotion during a time when your grandmother had been brought to be questioned by my aunt, and she was able to escape her guards.' His expression darkened. 'Though there was no proof the guards had been part of it, my aunt had them all stripped of their positions and cast out of the guild. That was why we had enforcers as guards, and different servants brought our meals each time. My aunt would have ensured their oath prevented them from talking to us and would not risk any of them becoming sympathetic to our plight.'

'There was no mention of the servant or anyone else helping her in the journal. Nor anything about secret messages.'

'Your grandmother probably feared it would be discovered. As personal as the entries in the journal are, they would reveal nothing other than her determination to win her freedom. She would not want to risk her supporters being discovered.'

That made sense, and Merry settled down to sleep that night thinking about how lonely her grandmother must have been, locked away for decades. But at least she had been buoyed up by the secret messages. Merry had experienced one week of loneliness. She could not have endured much more of it.

Her link with Sadie was a constant and comforting presence in the back of her head. She had been her grandmother's companion, but they had been separated in mind as well as body for years.

It was a bleak existence. I remained near the tower, ever vigilant for a way to get to Meredith. It would have been better to be by her side, even though it would be impossible for us to communicate telepathically, than to endure that dreadful silence. I felt as if half my soul was missing. The joy when I once again felt the touch of her mind, after so many years of silence, was indescribable.

The black cat sauntered to Merry's side. *I tried to follow you, when the healers carried you to the tower, but Ellen's dratted enforcer stopped me. I made him pay dearly for it.* Savage glee rang in her mental voice. *I sank my teeth into his hand as deep as I could, but he refused to let go until it was too late.* Sadie's eyes narrowed as she eyed Ellen. *She wanted to heal him, but I would not have it. If he was the reason I lost my companion, for a second time, he would suffer the consequences.*

Thank you. Merry stroked her silky soft fur. *You are the best companion any mage could ever have.*

Sadie let out a soft meow. *Yes, I am.* Then she closed her eyes and nestled into Merry's side, a soft purr lifting from her warm body.

'Beethoven and I will take first watch,' said Gabriel, stepping away from the fire. He settled into the tree-line, propping his back up against a large trunk. Content that she was safe for the moment, Merry let Sadie's purr lull her to sleep.

It felt as if she had just closed her eyes when Gabriel gently shook her awake.

'Is it my turn to watch?' Merry struggled into a sitting position, realising Sadie was no longer snuggled into her side. She frowned as she realised she could see Gabriel's face clearly though the fire had died down. The pale light of dawn wreathed through the tree canopy.

'You should have woken me.'

He shook his head as he stepped back, holding out a hand to help her to rise from her bedroll. 'You needed the sleep more than I did. I didn't expend half as much magic as you did to get us clear of the guild.' He smiled softly. 'I'm also not the one still recovering from magical exhaustion.'

'I'm fine. There's no need to coddle me.' Merry combed her fingers through her tangled hair, sure she must look a mess.

'The guild healers did a marvellous job, but not even they are able to perform miracles. You almost died, Merry.' He stepped closer, grey eyes shimmering with emotion. 'I was terrified we would not make it to the tower in time, and the healers would fail to save you. I'm beyond glad that was not the case, but I ask that you permit me to indulge in a small amount of coddling until I am assured of your full recovery.'

Spoken like that, there was little Merry could do but acquiesce. 'I'm taking a turn at watch tonight,' she said as she gave him a smile, blushing at the depth of feeling in his gaze. He was so handsome, kind and honourable. Her body tingled at the memory of being as one with him, and the amazing kiss they'd shared, when their minds had been linked together at the Water focal point. With her collapse and subsequent imprisonment by the guild, there had been no time to discuss the kiss or the way they felt about each other. Now wasn't the time to talk about it either.

As Gabriel moved off, Merry looked over to where Ellen was busy rolling up her bedroll. The rest of the healer's belongings were already packed, as was the food. They'd let her sleep to the last minute, and it was a sign of how tired she'd been that she hadn't heard them moving about. She rolled up her bedroll before moving off into the trees to empty her bladder. When she returned to the camp, she accepted a parcel of food from Ellen with a grateful smile.

Conscious of time passing, Merry ate the small bread roll as they walked. Ellen had slathered it with a sweet fruit paste that tingled on her tastebuds, making her wonder what herbs or spells had gone into the making. She washed it down with a few sips from her waterskin, fresh energy washing away the lingering lethargy from her deep sleep. Her muscles ached from the exertion of the day before, but Merry took that as a good sign. Soon she would be as fit as she had been before succumbing to magical exhaustion at the Water focal point.

There was little conversation as they walked. Merry sure her friends were just as concerned about possible pursuit or being spotted by those who would report their whereabouts to the guild as she was. Twice they had to backtrack due to dense forest blocking their way and she begrudged each setback. Around midday they reached a small creek, stopping to eat lunch and to refill their waterskins. They did not linger, though the spot they had stopped in was beautiful and inviting.

So much of Tirana was like this, green and peaceful, unlike the sun-baked land Merry was accustomed to back in Australia. Not that her home didn't have its own beauty. It was just nice to walk and not worry about getting fried to a crisp by a harsh sun or to hazard stumbling across one of the many venomous snakes and spiders that abounded in the Australian bush. At least, she didn't think there were any like that here.

Nature here does have its perils, but snakes are not one of them, and our spiders are harmless for the most part.

Merry narrowed her eyes at Sadie's words. *For the most part?*

There is a highly venomous species of spider, the infernae, but as they were a result of an experiment by a foolish mage their numbers are few. There was a campaign to eradicate them decades ago. It is highly unlikely any survived.

Highly unlikely was not impossible, and Merry's skin crawled at the thought of encountering one of them.

Any spider that was the creation of a foolish experiment was not one she ever wanted to have dealings with. But considering the amount of dangers and magical catastrophes she had encountered so far she glumly considered the odds not to be in her favour.

She scanned the underbrush around her carefully for spiderwebs, slowing her pace as she went.

Relax, Merry, these spiders prefer a warmer, more humid climate. The forest does not suit their nature at all, considering they were created by a Fire mage.

Merry stiffened, a horrible thought entering her head. *Please don't tell me the Fire focal point is in a warm and humid climate.*

The grotto that contains the Fire focal point is situated within a dormant volcano, on the coastline of Seahaven Province. There are many hot springs surrounding it, so yes, the climate is warm and humid.

Stifling a groan, Merry was about to ask how did one kill one of those spiders, when Gabriel held up a hand to indicate for them to stop and be silent. Heart pounding, Merry listened carefully, intent to see what it was he had discovered. He was pointing ahead of them to a gap between the trees. As she peered through the gap, she spotted movement on the other side.

Wait here. Beethoven and I will scout ahead. Without waiting for Merry's response, both cats bounded forward and quickly disappeared.

They returned a short time later, lithe bodies tense.

Two squads of enforcers are guarding the pass.

Beethoven stood beside Sadie, but his green gaze was on Gabriel as he spoke.

In a whisper, Merry repeated the familiar's words for Ellen's benefit.

The healer gave a low gasp. 'Is Adrian with them?'

The grey and white cat shook his head, ears twitching.

'How did they get here before us?' Gabriel asked.

From what we overheard they were already enroute before your escape. It seems your aunt had given the order to block all routes into Andelmine Province, even before she had the full approval of the mage council to do so. Last night, they chased off a group that sought to get past them. I believe it to be the same ones that fled the citadel and who have the heartstones.

Though relieved the black-haired man had not been able to get into Andelmine this way and was further delayed in getting the heartstones to Andel to enslave Britta and the others, that left Merry and her friends with a new dilemma. The main pass would also be well guarded, meaning they had no way of getting to the manor to free the others.

What were they going to do now?

CHAPTER 6

*W*ith Gabriel in the lead and taking care where they placed their feet to avoid making noise, Merry and her friends retreated through the trees as fast as they dared. Merry had half her attention on where they were headed, and the other half scanning behind them with her Earth sense to make sure they weren't being followed. Once they were out of earshot they sped up, increasing the distance between them and the pass.

After an hour, Gabriel signalled a stop. 'Do you still have your map, Ellen?'

Ellen nodded and rummaged in her pack for the map Mistress Napally had given them when she and Merry had been on their way to the Earth focal point.

Gabriel placed the map on the ground, weighing it down with twigs, and then crouched to point at a squiggly line. 'This is where we are now, and here is the pass.'

On the map, the distance between the two spots was close enough to make Merry nervous. Maybe they should keep going. They hadn't hidden their tracks and despite her regular scanning, she worried she had missed something. If the guards at the pass had an Earth mage with them, their presence could have been discovered and their trail would be easy to follow.

When she pointed out the danger, Gabriel gave a nod. 'We will not linger here for long. But we do need to come up with a new plan.'

He pointed to a new spot on the map, this one to the left of where he'd said they were, with what appeared to be a range of mountains between them. 'This is where Lord Andel's manor is located. It has been some time since I travelled in this section of the province, but from memory I believe there is an old road that used to connect Andelmine with Windemere's Province through the range. It could still be passable.'

'Windemere? Isn't that the count who was looking to annex part of Rangaleemore Province?' Merry explained how she had overheard him talking to his enforcers when she had first arrived in Tirana and had been on the run from him.

Gabriel's eyebrows rose and he huffed out a laugh. 'I had no idea you were hiding so close by.' Then his expression sobered. 'Yes. Count Windemere has been vocal in his desire to gain more territory. Lord Rangalee is not a forceful man, and when we arrived Windemere was attempting to broker a deal that would see him cede temporary control to part of his province in return for protection from bandits. Bandits that I believe are truly a squad of Windemere's men. I feared if Rangalee agreed, he would soon discover that the loan of land would not turn out to be temporary after all. I was able to dissuade him from signing.'

'Sounds as if this Windemere guy is as bad as Lord Andel,' said Merry. What was it with nobles who think they were entitled to take whatever they wanted?

'Yes, although he prefers to do deals with those who may not look too closely at the fine print than to resort to violence. There are rumours he also believes a return to the monarchy would be in Tirana's interests. He has no love for Andel, thanks to a feud between their families that goes back many generations. His approach is that a true king should be nominated by and then elected from the nobility, with himself acting as a steward until the election could take place. Which of course, is a post I would not see him giving up easily.'

Merry shook her head. 'He sounds horrible, but if there is a way to get to Andelmine from his province, then I guess going there is our best bet.'

Break time over, they set off. The day was cool, wind whipping the hem of Merry's cloak around her heels, each gust reminding her that winter was fast approaching. The need to hurry kept her going through the day, and her companions must have felt the same urgency as no one suggested stopping to eat. Instead Ellen parcelled out food to them as they walked.

They travelled as far as they could, continuing on as dusk settled in around them, only stopping when true night fell, and it became hard to see. Conscious of not wanting to draw attention, they found a sheltered copse to spend the night in far from any habitation. As she gazed at the small fire Gabriel had built so Ellen could warm their meal, Merry wondered what she would find at the Fire focal point, after she had completed the side quest.

The flames danced in the fire pit, steadily consuming the twigs and branches to keep it alight. A mix of colours, their movement was mesmerising and Merry felt her body still, her heart rate slow. But while it may have helped put her in a meditative state, there was no indication the flames stirred any Fire ability in her body.

At the Air, Earth and Water focal points, she'd had to draw on their elements to complete the challenges to gain her charms. Each time it had been desperation and instinct that had guided her actions. It would be nice, for once, to already know how to handle an element before it became a life and death situation.

She persevered, but by the time their food was ready, Merry still hadn't been able to connect with the Fire element. Maybe the others were wrong in thinking she would be able to master all five elements? She had been able to see the ghosts in the haunted Spirit enclave of Ralinin, and she had felt the call of the Spirit focal point while she had been at the guild tower, so she should be able to master Spirit. Fire was an unknown element but a vital one if she were to create the transportation spell that would allow her to return to her world.

As she snuggled into her bedroll later that night, making herself as comfortable as she could and with Sadie nestled into her side, Merry hoped her friends hadn't been wrong about her.

This time, Gabriel woke Merry for her turn at watch. Though tempted to see if she could sense anything from the embers in the fire, she focused her attention on her surroundings. Her fear that they might have been followed had lessened with time and distance between them and the guards at the pass, but she periodically scanned for signs anyone else was nearby. It would not be good to let her attention lapse. They were being hunted by enforcers, and the black-haired man and his crew would also be searching for a way into Andelmine Province. This was no time to get mesmerised by flames.

Her watch passed uneventfully, and she gratefully returned to her bedroll when Ellen took her turn.

When dawn came, they were already up and packed, setting off as soon as it was light enough to do so.

The day passed slowly, a repeat of the one before, and Merry was glad when the terrain changed, the ground beginning to rise as they drew closer to the mountain range that separated Windemere from Andelmine. The grass underfoot became sporadic, and the trees were spaced farther apart as the day passed. Late in the afternoon Gabriel announced they were nearing the old road that would lead them to Andelmine, and Merry spotted the remains of an old stone building up ahead. She was in the lead as they edged around the ruin and then froze.

Dozens of militias composed of men and women in dark brown and gold uniforms, were in the process of setting up a rudimentary camp beside the ruins. While many were intent on their tasks, more were standing facing Merry and her friends. She turned to flee, cursing herself for being more focused on sensing behind them than ahead, but it was too late. More militia streamed out of the ruins to block their path.

As the militia closed in, Merry and her friends stood back-to-back, and she gripped her staff. With a deep breath, she felt within herself for the spark of her Air magic, ready to whip up a whirlwind to create a barrier at the first sign the militia were about to attack. Most of them carried swords, but a few had bows with arrows ready to be let loose. She would not let them harm Ellen and Gabriel, or the cats.

'I demand to speak to whoever is in charge here.' Gabriel's voice was firm, showing no sign he was bothered by being surrounded by armed militia.

'Demand all you like,' one of the militia men said with a sneer. 'Don't mean you'll get what you want.'

'Harris, you're on latrines duty. Go.' A tall woman

with short brown hair strode over from the camp and glared at the man who had sneered at Gabriel.

'But Captain—'

'Unless you want it to be a permanent post, you need to go. Now.'

The militiaman blanched and took off at a run, while the captain turned to face Gabriel. 'I apologise for my man's rudeness, Mage Fairweather. He likely didn't recognise you. It is not often we see mages without their robes.' Her gaze travelled down Gabriel's lean form, making it apparent she liked what she saw. Then she lifted her gaze to his face. 'If you had informed us of your intent to visit Windemere, the count would have arranged a suitable escort for you.' Now her gaze flicked dismissively over Merry and Ellen.

'It is no concern, Captain Trevally, and I apologise for bursting in on your camp like this without informing Count Windemere. We had not expected to find ourselves venturing this way.'

Relieved though she was that they had not stumbled into the hands of Andel's militia, Merry still did not relax her grip on her staff. This Captain Trevally, for all her apparent courtesy toward Gabriel, had not ordered the rest of her troops to stand down. They were still ringed around them, the archers with arrows at the ready.

But again, Gabriel showed no sign of concern in his manner as he continued, 'We were merely seeking a way to cross into Andelmine. We have urgent business there.'

'I would not expect a mage such as yourself to embark on guild business with only two witches as escort. Last time you visited us, as I recall, you had a squad of enforcers with you.' Captain Trevally's tone was arch, one dark eyebrow rising as she rested a hand on her hip.

'Our enforcers are preoccupied with other tasks, but I can assure you my friends are a more than adequate escort,' said Gabriel, his tone conversational. Then he inclined his head. 'If you will excuse us, Captain, we have far to travel before nightfall.'

Her other eyebrow rose, and she gave a fake gasp. 'Why, Mage Fairweather, you intend to take your leave of us so soon? I am sure Count Windemere would be disappointed to learn he missed another chance to dine with you. Surely your … business … for the guild could wait one more day.'

Gabriel scanned the camp. 'Count Windemere is here?'

Captain Trevally shook her head. 'Not yet, but we are expecting him to arrive within the hour. Come,' she said as she stepped to the side and waved a hand for Gabriel to walk ahead of her. 'You and your … friends … can rest in the command tent while we wait for the count and his escort to arrive.'

Gabriel advises we do as the captain asks. We could insist on leaving, but if it came to a fight it could prove more costly than a small delay. Beethoven tilted his head, green eyes slitted as he looked up at Merry. *If it proves necessary, we will extricate ourselves from the situation when the guards are not so vigilant.*

Merry signalled her assent, and Gabriel soon strode off to where a large gold tent was in the process of being erected. Captain Trevally was at his side. Merry and Ellen followed them, with Sadie and Beethoven weaving their way around the edges of the ruin, staying in the shadows.

Merry saw Captain Trevally turn to watch them, and she silently cautioned both familiars to be careful.

At the tent, Captain Trevally barked orders until a number of wooden folding chairs and a table were placed inside. Then she ushered Gabriel and the others into the tent. More of the militia bustled in and out, setting up a lush bed. Once the militia had finished their tasks, the captain urged Gabriel, Merry and Ellen to sit, taking a seat herself at the table.

'Please, you must be tired after your journey. Or perhaps, you have not travelled far.' The captain eyed their bedrolls and laden packs, now placed against the wall of the tent. 'You seem well prepared for a sojourn in the woods. Though as I said before, it is strange to see a mage not wearing his robes or escorted by enforcers. Dare I ask, is this supposed to be clandestine business you are engaged in? Walking into an armed camp is not the hallmark of any spy I have ever heard of.'

'I assure you, Captain Trevally, we are not here to spy. As I said we merely have business to attend to in

Andelmine. But I am afraid, this is not business I can discuss with those not part of the guild.'

'Since when are witches part of the guild?'

'The young ladies are training to be mages and, as for our attire, mage robes can be more of a hindrance when travelling on foot, always tangling on branches.'

Captain Trevally gave a soft snort and then got to her feet. 'Enjoy your rest. I will inform the count of your presence as soon as he arrives.' Then she strode out of the tent and could be heard barking more orders at her troops.

Ellen went to speak and Merry shook her head. Just because they were alone in the tent didn't mean there was no one listening outside. She reached out with her Earth senses and found four guards stationed within earshot around the tent. She held up a hand with four fingers raised, even as she telepathically asked Beethoven to inform Gabriel of their audience.

Gabriel gave a nod, and then started an innocuous conversation with her and Ellen, even as his response came from Beethoven that they would have to wait until Windemere arrived before they planned what they would do. Luckily, they did not have to wait long before Sadie warned Merry that the count had arrived, and a moment later she heard a commotion outside the tent. Merry tensed but took her cue from Gabriel, who remained seated, calmly waiting for whatever would happen next.

A murmured conversation, too low for individual

words to be understood, took place outside the tent. Then the door was cast aside and a short man with balding blond hair entered the tent with Captain Trevally at his back. Two more militia guards entered behind them and took up positions to either side of the door. A whisper of goosebumps crossed Merry's skin, and she didn't believe it was coming from either of her friends.

She scanned the militia and one of them, a woman with black hair twisted into a neat bun, stared back at her. The woman's chin was raised, the look in her brown eyes defiant. She flushed when Gabriel twisted in his seat and gazed upon her.

'It appears Lord Andel is not the only noble to employ magic users, though I hope your methods of recruitment are not as drastic as his,' said Gabriel, as he stood and bowed in the direction of the man who had to be Count Windemere.

The count gave a bark of a laugh, a wide smile creasing his face as he stepped forward and clapped Gabriel on the shoulder. 'Well spotted, Mage Fair-weather. I should have known my bodyguard's affinity for magic would not escape your keen eye. I hope you will forgive Torres for not wearing her colours. They clash with the uniform.'

Merry was sure the apparent clash of colours had nothing to do with why Torres was not wearing clothing that indicated which of the elemental magics she had an affinity for, and everything to do with the count wishing to keep hidden the fact his bodyguard was anything other than standard militia.

Merry scanned the other guard, wondering if he was also a magic user. His eyes narrowed with suspicion as he gazed back at her, so much like the looks Adrian had sent her way, that she wouldn't be surprised to discover he was telekinetic. Unlike an elemental ability, that had no tell-tale like the goosebumps that Merry was aware of.

'Refreshments will be served soon,' said Count Windemere, giving Gabriel a jovial smile. 'Sit with us and let us enjoy a humble repast while you tell me why you wish to journey into Andelmine. Without being detected, I presume.' He sat heavily into the empty chair beside Merry, while Captain Trevally took the seat she had occupied earlier.

Count Windemere gave Merry a wink and then nodded his head towards Gabriel. 'You did not have such delightful company when I saw you last. Instead of enforcers we have a healer from Dryton, and a newly discovered witch of the Meadows bloodline.'

Gabriel's expression remained even, as he inclined his head in the count's direction. 'You are well informed, my lord.'

'Please, Mage Fairweather. There is no need to be so formal. Call me Zachary and do introduce me properly to your lovely companions.'

Gabriel made the introductions, no sign in his tone that he was discomfited by the Count knowing who they were. There was a polite murmur of greetings around the table as four more militia entered carrying laden plates and mugs. They silently set them on the table, and then bowed towards the count before leaving the tent.

The count urged them to eat and drink, and then immediately tucked into his own meal.

Merry cast a sideways glance at Ellen, then looked down at the plate in front of her. It held what looked like roast beef, potatoes and vegetables, all swimming in a rich gravy, while the mug appeared to hold chicory flavoured coffee. It all smelled delicious, but she waited as her friend clasped the heartstone tucked away in her bodice, and tell-tale goosebumps rose on her arms. When Ellen gave a nod, she happily began to eat. She was not going to let the hard gazes of Torres and her partner, as well as that of Captain Trevally, put her off her meal.

As they ate, the count reminisced with Gabriel about their encounter in Rangaleemore and the outcome of that meeting, Windemere laughing off his attempt to annex part of the neighbouring province.

'You will have Miss Hayland here believing me to be a monster, Gabriel, one eager to gobble up her home. But I assure you,' he said as he turned to her, 'all I wanted to do was ensure that my neighbour was not taken advantage of by bandits and the like who prey on the unwary and helpless.'

'I hardly see Lord Rangalee as unwary or helpless,

Count Windemere,' said Ellen with an arch tone. 'He has ruled our province fairly and conscientiously since he became head of the family.'

'That he has, and it is good you are loyal to him,' said the count with an easy smile. 'And please, no more Count Windemere. You make me sound old and stuffy. I prefer to be informal when dining with friends, don't I, Captain Trevally?'

'As you say, my lord.' Trevally, who had barely touched the food on offer, seeming to prefer to sip slowly at her coffee, had a tone as arch as Ellen's had been.

The plate before him now empty, the count picked up his mug as he eyed Gabriel for a long moment. Then, with no trace of a smile on his face or in his voice, he said, 'Andel must be stopped. To have him proclaimed as king would be a disaster for all Tirana. I hope your presence here, with what is rumoured to be the witch who has already bested him twice, means the guild is ready to move against him.'

Gabriel, who had placed down his mug, said, 'I am not at liberty to discuss guild business with outsiders, but I can assure you the guild has no intention of seeing Tirana return to a monarchy, no matter which faction seeks a crown that no longer exists.'

'There are those who believe the guild's management of Tirana is no longer advantageous,' said the count. 'They believe it is time for new management to take over, be that a monarchy or some other form of governance.'

'They would be mistaken.' Gabriel's tone was the hardest Merry had ever heard it and it seemed Count Windemere was also taken aback by his commitment to the guild remaining in charge.

But he swiftly rallied. 'Am I to take it then, that your current mission pertains to Andel's claim to that non-existent crown of yours?'

'All I am permitted to say, is that our mission would serve no good to Lord Andel's cause. If you truly have the best interests of all Tirana at heart, then you would allow my companions and me safe passage into Andelmine so we may continue our journey.'

Count Windemere, for there was no way Merry could think of him as Zachary, looked over to where Torres stood against the wall. The ripple of goosebumps signalled magic being used nearby, and the young woman's lips moved slightly as she whispered her spell. Merry felt pressure in her head, not as invasive as when she had been attacked by Spirit mages previously but enough that it left no doubt which element Torres had an affinity for.

Merry instantly formed an image of a brick wall in her mind, placing it in front of Gabriel, Ellen and herself, imagining the woman's mental probe being deflected harmlessly. The pressure in her head increased so Merry added iron spikes to her wall, imagining them piercing the flesh of anyone attempting to get near.

Torres grimaced, and the pressure in Merry's head vanished. Still, the goosebumps continued for a long and drawn-out moment.

Then the count waved a hand. 'Enough, Torres. If you have not been able to glean any information from them by now then you are outmatched.'

As the goosebumps subsided, the count turned to Merry. 'I don't suppose you care to cast aside this mission of yours and join my humble band?'

Merry met his eyes. 'No.'

He huffed out a laugh and turned to Gabriel. 'If your mission will hurt Andel's ambitions, then I gladly offer you safe passage. I will have a tent set aside for your use, and in the morning Captain Trevally will lead you to the pass that will allow you to enter Andelmine without notice.'

He stood up. 'Now, if you will excuse me, I must confer with the good captain regarding our own mission.'

Merry rose, as did Gabriel and Ellen. There was no chance to grab their packs as the four militias standing guard outside the tent entered and ushered them out.

As they were led to a nearby tent and told to make themselves comfortable, Merry hoped the count would keep his word, as his arrival had doubled the amount of militia they would face if it came to a fight, and she had to wonder how many of them had a hidden ability like Torres.

CHAPTER 7

*A*fter a night spent tossing and turning, fearing Torres would try to burrow into her mind while she slept, Merry was more than ready to leave Windemere's camp behind once morning arrived.

The four guards from the night before had been changed, though the new ones were no more welcoming than the last lot when Merry emerged from the tent alongside Ellen. This group was all male, making Merry grateful when Torres arrived with two female militia and announced she was there to escort them to the latrines. As they walked the short distance from the camp, Torres cast frequent glances at Merry.

Once they had all used the latrine, and left the smelly site behind, Torres indicated for Merry to stop walking. Ellen stopped also, but the other guards urged her to continue on to camp. When the healer cast a worried glance at Merry, she indicated to her friend that she was fine. With a nod, Ellen allowed the guards to lead her on.

Merry watched her walk away, waiting for Torres to broach whatever it was that was weighing on her mind. The other woman didn't speak until Ellen and the others were far enough away that they wouldn't overhear.

'Do you think Mage Fairweather will report me to the guild? I don't want to be a guild mage. I never wanted that. Please don't make me go to the tower.' Torres' brow was furrowed, shoulders hunched forward, and arms crossed in front of her chest. 'I'll never get to see my family again. None of them have the strength to become mages.'

Merry shook her head. 'Gabriel is not interested in recruiting for the guild, and I'd be the last person to force anyone to join them. As far as I'm concerned, no one has the right to stop you from seeing your family, and whether you choose to become a mage or not is up to you.'

As Torres straightened, up, the haunted look in her eyes vanishing, Merry added, 'But that doesn't mean you can go around using your magic to hurt people. You need to stay out of people's minds uninvited, and don't use your magic to harm others.'

Torres snorted. 'I'm the count's bodyguard. Snooping and using my magic to protect him is part of the job.'

'There's a big different between self-defence and deliberately trying to hurt someone else.' Merry shuddered at the memory of the times Spirit magic had been used as a weapon against her, and of what she had been forced to do to protect herself and others as a result. 'If you are ever in a situation where the count or anyone else asks you to harm another person for no good reason, and you do it, that's when we would have a problem.'

Torres pursed her lips, nodding slowly. 'The count is a good leader, but I will be careful. I don't want to hurt people unless they give me no choice.' She turned and led the way back to the tent to where Gabriel and Ellen stood beside Count Windemere, all their packs and belongings on the ground before them.

Captain Trevally was nearby with the guards who had been on duty the night before.

Count Windemere gave Merry a welcoming smile as she joined her friends. 'Good morning, Miss Meadows. I hope you slept well and are refreshed for the next step in your journey to be a thorn in Lord Andel's side.'

'Thank you for your hospitality, Count Windemere,' she said, before scooping up her staff.

Windemere's smile widened. 'The good captain is determined to see you on your way so she can return to her duties, so I will bid you farewell. My cooks have prepared food for your journey. Mage Fairweather has informed me you may not be the only ones seeking a way into Andelmine. He also tells me Lord Andel will be displeased if these others are delayed. If I see them, you can be assured I will do my best to halt their progress. I wish you success in your endeavours. Any mission that seeks to irk Lord Andel has my full blessing.' He inclined his head.

Captain Trevally cleared her throat. 'This way,' she said before striding off, setting a fast pace as she wove her way through the tents. Merry and her friends grabbed their packs and hurriedly followed, with a squad of Windemere's militia at their backs.

Before Merry had taken a dozen steps, Sadie and Beethoven streaked forth from the ruins, winding their way through the legs of the marching militia to reach her and Gabriel.

Trevally's head turned to follow the familiars, but she said nothing, and her pace didn't slow as they left the camp behind and passed beyond the last of the ruined buildings. Rubble was strewn among the grass, showing the remains of what had once been a stone wall. They picked their way carefully, not wanting to turn an ankle on the camouflaged stones. Merry was once again grateful she had been wearing her black ankle books when she had unknowingly triggered that spell that transported her and Sadie to Tirana.

According to Ellen, they were two days walk from Dryton; two days away from the portal she would need to use to return home. Not that it would do her any good until she had the Fire and Spirit charms. Still, the knowledge that she was so close to it, and was instead walking off in the other direction, chafed. Was she doing the right thing, insisting on freeing Britta and the other captured witches? Would her time be better served heading to the Fire focal point and getting her charm?

But if Andel succeeded in adding to his army of enslaved witches, their oaths unwillingly bound by the perverted heartstones, he would surely march against the guild. That would mean there would be no one free to fight off the witch hunters if they managed to get through the portal. She had to stay the course. Tirana needed to have a stable government in place and not be involved in a civil war if she was not able to get home and renew the wards around the portal in time.

A chill wind snaked around them as they marched closer to a low mountain range, remnants of the broken wall marking their path. They no longer needed Trevally to lead the way, but she made no move to turn back. As they arrowed towards a dark gap between two ridges, the militia guards closed in around her small group and Merry wondered if they had been foolish to believe Windemere was going to let them pass through to Andelmine. But then, if he had intended to betray them, he could have done it back at his camp. Even with magic on their side, she and Gabriel would have been hard pressed to fight off so many.

A moment later Trevally called a halt, and turned to face Gabriel, the looming ridges casting shadows over her features. 'It has been a number of years since this path was last taken by any of our number, but it has stood for many generations. If you follow the wall, it will lead you through the ridges. Walk until the wall ends, and then take a further one hundred paces forward. Then, look to the cliff face on your left and you will find the opening to a tunnel, hidden behind a stand of oak trees.'

With that she stepped back and indicated for her guards to return the way they had come.

Neither Merry nor the others moved or spoke until Trevally and the guards were out of sight. Even then, Merry waited until she had cast out her senses to assure herself that none of them remained hidden just around the bend. Then she focused on the way forward, delving her senses deep into the cliff face on the left until she found the tunnel Trevally had referred to. Her consciousness travelled deep within the mountain range, finding no obstacles as far as her Earth magic would allow her to see, and no sign of anyone else nearby.

She pulled her senses back and faced her friends. 'The tunnel is there, and it appears to be going in the right direction, but my magic can't reach the other side.'

Gabriel gave a nod. 'I don't believe Windemere was lying about the pass going all the way to Andelmine, but either way we have no choice but to continue. If we are to reach the imprisoned witches before they are oath bound to obey Andel, this is our best chance.'

He was right, and between them they should have the ability to overcome any obstacles that arose. They followed the stone wall to its end, and then Merry led the way to the oak trees hiding the tunnel. Large fronded ferns with spikes on the ends partially obscured the entrance and she used her magic to ease them aside, releasing them once she and her friends were on the other side. The tunnel was dark, the floor covered in twigs, dead leaves and dirt, the opening wide enough to allow a cart through. None of them were in danger of banging their heads on the ceiling.

Merry commanded her staff to light up and then strode inside. After getting caught out at the ruins, she kept a hand on the left wall, her senses roaming farther ahead of them as they walked. Ellen and Gabriel, without staffs, used lanterns loaned to them by Windemere to aid their progress, while Sadie and Beethoven had no trouble navigating the semi darkness. As they ventured on, the ground cleared of leaf debris and dirt, though there was no indication that was because of human intervention. More likely it was because the wind would not reach this far in. Merry's senses gave no hint of anyone living within the mountain— unlike the case of the one where she had encountered the Singers.

Thinking of them, and the heartstones they nourished with their songs, made Merry wonder who the black-haired man working for Lord Andel was. He must have Singer blood, to be able to rejuvenate the broken ones and use them to bind oaths. Thanks to having a Singer for a grandfather, she had been able to use damaged heartstones when she held them. Their effectiveness ceased the moment she stopped touching them. The man appeared to be capable of much more, so perhaps his father or mother had been a Singer. He appeared to be around her parents' age. He was way too young to have been the man who dallied with her grandmother decades earlier.

No, he had to be like her, with a Singer parent or grandparent, or maybe he was a full Singer who had left the mountain behind. All the ones she had seen had white hair. There hadn't even been any light brown or blonde. Black would have stood out immediately. She reminded herself she shouldn't assume that those she had seen had been the full extent of the Singer race based on such a short time with them.

She shook these thoughts off, to focus on her task at hand. All going well she would never have to encounter the black-haired man again.

The trek through the tunnel was long and slow. The air was still, dust stirred up by their passage. By the time they stopped to rest and eat lunch, Merry's head pounded from using her Earth magic to sense ahead. She gratefully accepted Ellen's offer to take over once they set off again. Ellen kept one hand on her heartstone and the other on the wall as they walked.

Two hours later, Ellen stopped a short distance from a bend. 'The tunnel has collapsed just ahead. I can't sense a way through.'

Merry groaned as she rounded the bend and saw the way was completely blocked, large rocks piled to the roof of the tunnel and scattered on the ground before it. She delved her senses through the rock pile.

'It goes for at least five metres, and I can't find another way through.' There had been no side tunnels along the way, though there had been small alcoves carved into the walls, perhaps used for rest breaks by weary travellers.

Ellen moved forward and placed a hand on one of the rocks jutting out of the pile. 'You're right. It appears the ceiling collapsed many years ago.' She turned back to face them. 'That would explain why there was no sign it has been used recently.'

'Do you think Windemere knew, when he had Captain Trevally lead us here?' Merry asked.

Gabriel shook his head. 'I don't believe he acted in bad faith. If he had wanted to stop us entering Andelmine, he could have taken us prisoner, or not told us there was a passage through.'

Merry wasn't so sure about that. The delay for them to backtrack and find a new way into Andelmine could cost them days. Maybe Windemere was not so averse to Andel being king after all, and this was his way of getting them out of the way so the black-haired man could get to Britta and the others before them.

She set her senses ranging, pushing her limits as far as she could go, and almost growled in frustration.

The opening for the tunnel was a short distance beyond the blockade. They were almost through. Worse, she could sense the sparks of many magical beings. As Windemere had promised, this tunnel would have led them straight to where Andel was holding the witches prisoner. So close, with only this stupid rock fall stopping them.

Merry scanned the nearby walls with her magic, hoping there would be small tunnels like the one they had used to escape Andel's militia near Greywall, though she winced at the memory of the ones who had been crushed when an earthquake had collapsed it on top of Andel's militia.

Here though, there were no such tunnels. No way out, other than to go back.

Unless…

Merry had not fully connected with her Earth magic back then. Could she use it now, to find a way through?

'I have an idea,' she said as she shucked off her pack so she could grip her staff with both hands. 'I'm going to try to move the rocks at the top to make a big enough gap for us to crawl through.'

Ellen nodded as she dropped her pack to the ground and reached up to place a hand on her heartstone pendant. 'If we work together, I'm sure we can do it.' She reached out her other hand and placed it on the rocks in front of them. 'I'm not as strong as you, so I'll start on this side.'

Merry gave a nod and moved to stand beside Ellen, reaching her senses through to the other end of the blockade, using her magic to urge the rocks to move. They were resistant to budging, having settled into place for so long, but she worked slowly, one rock at a time. A slow rumble came as Ellen worked on the rocks in front of them, and grit stung her eyes when one of them shifted and rolled down to the tunnel floor. Then a cool wind whipped around her, cooling her heated flesh and whisking the dirt and dust away. The scent of Gabriel's Air magic floated in the air, keeping her and Ellen clear of dust and debris.

Merry's shoulders slumped as she worked, dimly away that Ellen had stopped some time ago. She had cleared the rocks halfway from the other side while the healer had made a good-sized dent on this side. There was still at least two metres left to go.

Enough. Sadie's words were accompanied by the presence of sharp teeth on Merry's ankle. The familiar didn't break the skin, just pressed down hard enough to wrest Merry's attention from her task. *You will exhaust yourself and have nothing left for when we leave the safety of the tunnel. You need to eat something, and then rest. We can continue tomorrow when your body is replenished.*

Merry didn't want to stop without the tunnel being cleared, but now that she had pulled her focus from her task she was aware of how stiff and sore her body was from being in the same position for so long. Her head also ached from performing magic for an extended period. She accepted the mug of magic water from Ellen with a grateful sigh and was even more pleased to see Gabriel had set up their bedrolls. She sank gratefully down on hers and sipped at her water, while Ellen parcelled out food.

The tunnel floor was hard and lumpy, even with the

padded bedroll, but Merry was too tired to care. In the morning she was the first up, ducking back down the tunnel, using her staff for light, to find the spot she and Ellen had carved out to serve as a makeshift bathroom, manipulating the rock to absorb her body waste. Then she returned to the camp and started working on the remaining blockage.

Merry had it cleared away before Ellen and Gabriel woke. After a quick meal, they secured their packs to their bodies for the crawl through the gap. Merry needed both hands free, so her staff was tied to her pack, meaning she would have no light. She had strengthened the rocks left behind, to make sure they did not shift as they climbed to the opening and then began the slow crawl through the tunnel she and Ellen had made.

Sadie and Beethoven clambered up with ease and quickly disappeared into the darkness.

Out of breath, hands and knees scraped raw and bruised on elbows and head by the time she made it to the end, Merry carefully manoeuvred down the rock pile and wove a path through the rocks she had displaced. The air was fresher on this side, the opening into the mountainside not far away, though no light penetrated. She was quick to untie her staff and shed light on this section, even as she moved to the wall and sensed ahead.

Behind her, she could hear Ellen and Gabriel making their way through the tunnel. Ahead of her, she could sense the bright sparks that were the familiars as they lithely journeyed to the tunnel exit and peered out. Neither of the cats moved beyond the opening as Sadie relayed what she saw to Merry.

Windemere's scouts were correct. The prison camp containing the witches is a short distance from Lord Andel's manor. The number of them meant he would have been unable to fit them all in his dungeon. The little cat's tone was sour as she mentioned the dungeon.

Smoke is rising from what appears to be many campfires. It seems he has a considerable force camped at his prison.

Merry let her senses roam, and though she could not 'see' fires, she could see the sparks of a large group of magical people in one area, while two rings that contained a mix of magic and non-magic people surrounded them. It appeared the prison was in the very centre of a camp that presumably contained armed militia as well as enslaved or rogue magic users. Getting to Britta and the others was not going to be easy.

But not impossible.

She and her friends had surmounted many obstacles since she had arrived in Tirana and she was determined to find a way to get past this one as well. For now she waited for her friends to reach her side and rearrange their packs.

'Here, let me heal you before we set off. If you are anything like me you will be aching all over,' said Ellen with a wry grin. She placed a hand on Merry's arm and warmth soon soothed away the aches and pains she had received while crawling through the gap in the rocks. Ellen then turned her ministrations to Gabriel.

Refreshed by the healer's magic, they set off for the tunnel exit and soon re-joined Sadie and Beethoven. The sun was edging over the horizon, as they stepped out and scanned their surroundings. There were more mountain ranges in the distance to the right of them, the ones where Britta and her people had been camped. The familiar guilt rippled through Merry, tempered by the knowledge she was about to attempt a rescue.

The tunnel exit was partway up the mountain, giving them a view of the tops of the forest that encompassed a large portion of Andelmine Province. Roads had been cut through, linking small townships, and a river snaked through the middle. She could see the grey roof of a large building, with cleared fields around it.

Lord Andel's manor. From this distance, she could not see if there was any activity there.

It was a different story to the left, halfway between them and the manor.

A great swathe of land had been cleared, the ground looking raw but not empty. The trees that had been chopped down had been used to build a prison camp. Several small tents were surrounded by high log walls. But it was the force arrayed around the outside of the circular prison camp that was more concerning. As Sadie had said, the smoke from numerous fires rose into the air and Merry could see the tops of dozens of tents.

Merry and her friends travelled down the mountainside, picking their way carefully, and she continued to scan ahead now they were in enemy territory. She would not be caught out again. Within a couple of hours they were making their way through the forest, parallel to the dirt road that led back towards Lord Andel's manor.

For the first time, her roving senses found signs of life nearby, and she signalled to her friends to halt. A short while later people appeared on the road, travelling from the manor with horse drawn wagons laden with supplies. None of the militia escorting the supply train, or the wagon drivers, shone with a magical light, but Merry still uttered a silent spell to keep herself and the others hidden.

They did not move off again until the supply train was ahead of them, and she continued to cast her spell as they followed along beside the road. Sadie and Beethoven streaked off through the trees, getting as close to the wagons as they dared, and what they reported back both reassured and alarmed Merry.

The guards were grumbling about the extra duties at the prison camp and hoping the Singer Lord Andel had employed arrived soon, so the witches could be oath bound and no longer need guarding. It was good to know the black-haired man had not yet arrived with his perverted heartstones, but bad when Sadie informed her who was in charge of the camp, and the main reason for the guards' dissatisfaction at their duty; Karl Piermont.

Merry shuddered at the thought of coming into

contact with the rogue enforcer who was also an Air mage. The last time she had come up against him he had almost killed her in his rage at her actions to thwart his schemes. From what she'd seen and experienced, the man was crazy and liable to do anything when angered. It was something she never wanted to see again.

But she would have to face him, or at least get dangerously close, if she were to have any hope of freeing Britta and the others.

She turned to face her companions and saw from Gabriel's expression that Beethoven had already informed him of what they would soon face. For Ellen's sake, she put it into words and watched the healer's cheeks pale.

Then Ellen squared her shoulders. 'You beat him before. You can do it again.'

Though heartened by her friend's words, Merry know it would not be as easy as that. Still, she continued onwards, hoping that when she got her first real look at the prison camp inspiration would strike.

$\mathcal{M}$erry held her invisibility spell in place as she and her friends crouched at the top of a rocky outcrop jutting out from the ground. They were at the edge of the forest, as close to the prison camp as they could get without being in the open. Her stomach knotted as she counted the tents encircling the actual prison. They were set out in an orderly fashion, with a wide space between the two rows. This space was filled with supplies and camp fires and appeared to be where the majority of the guards spent their time when not on duty. The tents were made from plain cream canvas, while coloured tents representing each of the elements were spaced evenly among them.

Armed militia patrolled the outer edge of the camp, and these were dressed in the familiar uniforms of Andelmine and Greystone. It was only a small relief to not see militia representing any of the other provinces. The number of coloured tents, and the magical sparks that said they were occupied by a mix of mages, witches and enforcers, meant it would be difficult if not impossible to sneak through the camp without being caught.

Merry turned her attention to the actual prison. The log walls formed a crude circle and left no corners to hide around, and the plain tents for the prisoners were bunched in the middle, meaning there was a wide gap between them and the wall. That gap meant any intruders or escaping prisoners would be easily spotted by the guards who stood on top of four platforms that loomed over the log wall. There were three guards in each one, and from the sparks that glowed in her Earth sense, she could tell that each post held two militia and one enforcer.

From her vantage point, Merry could see only one way in and out of the prison, a gate that faced the largest of the tents in the first row surrounding it. This tent was a dark red, and two militia guards in Greystone uniforms stood to either side of the open flap. With her magic, Merry could sense two people inside the tent. One spark was the familiar one of an enforcer. The other was a mix of red and white, the white blazing so brightly the individual had to be a mage.

There was only one person Merry knew that was both an enforcer and an Air mage.

Karl Piermont.

Heat flooded her body and her pulse pounded in her ears when Karl strode out of the tent. He no longer wore the red robe but was decked out in a silver tunic that shimmered with each movement. Red piping ran down the sides of his black trousers, and a white cloak hung from his shoulders. His bearing was confident, assured of his own power, and Merry clenched her jaw as she watched him talk to one of the guards. As Karl re-entered the red tent, the guard ran to the next one, a cream one, and poked his head in through the flap. A short time later he escorted Captain Baldwin, leader of Lord Andel's militia, over to Karl's tent.

Captain Baldwin entered as the guard returned to his post, and within seconds a woman in an enforcer's red robe stepped out of the tent and strode off through the camp. Her head was bowed, but there was no mistaking that it was Karl's sister, Kassandra. Without looking around, the dark-haired enforcer made her way to a small red tent behind Karl's and slipped inside.

Sadie nudged Merry's side. *Whatever you plan on doing, I suggest you do it fast. If Karl finds out we are here, it will prove impossible to free the witches without getting caught.*

I know.

The thought of what would happen if Karl caught them set Merry's stomach churning. She had been lucky to escape last time. Part of that luck had included Kassandra helping them. The first inkling of an idea appeared.

Beethoven and I will keep watch, while you three figure out how we are to achieve the impossible. Again.

Merry turned to face Gabriel and Ellen. Both of them wore grave expressions, appearing as daunted by what they faced as she was. With gestures, she indicated that they should retreat to the safety of the forest. She kept her 'do not see us, do not hear us' litany going until they were well hidden, and then carefully scanned their surroundings to verify no one was nearby before speaking.

'Kassandra Piermont helped Ellen and me escape from Karl back at the Marshland Dam. If we can convince her to help us, she might know a way for us to free Britta and the others before the man with the heartstones gets here.'

Gabriel frowned. 'Kassandra is a traitor to the guild. I know she helped you before, but she can't be trusted.'

'I agree, but we are running out of time. The quickest way for us to free Britta and the others would be with inside help.'

'Kassandra is terrified of her brother,' said Ellen. 'I think that's the only reason she is still with him. If we offered to help her get free of him, she might help us again.'

'You said he wanted her oath to the guild broken, and for her to swear a new one to obey him. What if that has already happened? We have no idea if that man we saw at the tower has been able to use one of his heartstones on her.' Gabriel shook his head. 'It is too risky. All it would take is one cry from her and Karl would set his people on us. Besides, she's in the middle of his camp. How would you even get to her, to ask for her help?'

'Kassandra knows Sadie. She could sneak into the camp tonight and get her attention.' Given the black cat's ability to make her intentions known to those she could not communicate with telepathically, Merry had no doubt Sadie would be able to get Kassandra to follow her out of camp.

I will take pleasure in nipping her ankles if she chooses to ignore my summons. Sadie's mental voice was sharp. *I will return with the enforcer soon.*

Hang on. We were still discussing if this was a good idea or not, and it's the middle of the day. You could be spotted.

What is there to discuss? You need assistance in freeing the witches. Kassandra has proved somewhat helpful in the past. And I can assure you, no one will see me unless I wish them to. Either way, we have no time to waste. That man with the heartstones could arrive at any moment, and then all hope of freeing these witches will be lost.

Merry winced as she faced Gabriel and Ellen. 'Sadie has gone to fetch Kassandra. She thinks time is of the essence and didn't want to wait until tonight.'

Gabriel sighed. 'Yes, Beethoven informed me of her decision. Now we need to decide what to do if Kassandra sounds the alarm.'

Here, Merry, see what I see.

At Sadie's words, Merry felt a slight tug in her head

and then her consciousness split in two. She was still standing in the shade of the trees with Gabriel and Ellen, but she was also approaching the camp, low to the ground, the scents of many people and horses filling her nose. Sadie was sharing her vision with her, as she had when Mage Fowler had attacked at the Earth focal point.

Merry closed her eyes to cut out the disorientation of seeing two things at once, and her sense of being mentally joined with Sadie strengthened as she/they slid through the first row of tents. She dimly heard Beethoven telepathically explaining to Gabriel what was happening, and he in turn told Ellen. Then she focused all her attention on what was happening in the camp.

Sadie was as silent as a shadow, slipping through the tents with ease, hugging the canvas and freezing whenever someone drew near. Soon she reached the tent into which Kassandra had disappeared. There were no guards posted here, and it was a quarter the size of the one Karl occupied. Sadie paused by the tent flap, edging her nose through the gap and scenting the air to confirm no one else was inside. Then she slipped through.

Kassandra was sitting on the edge of a camp bed, head in her hands, shoulders shaking and the muffled sounds of sobs coming from her. There was no one else in the tent with the enforcer, the only other furniture was a small table, a chair and a wooden trunk.

The familiar sauntered farther into the tent and jumped lightly onto the end of the camp bed, her movements assured. Then she reached out a paw and tapped Kassandra on the side of her face. The enforcer's head shot up; reddened eyes wide as she spotted Sadie. She gave a strangled gasp, one hand covering her mouth, while Sadie responded by delicately washing her paw.

Kassandra's eyes narrowed as she lowered her hand. 'She's here, isn't she?'

Sadie blinked slowly and then jumped down from the camp bed and went to the flap. Then she stopped and looked over her shoulder at Kassandra.

'No. I am not getting involved. Not again. Karl will kill me.' Her voice broke on the last few words.

Merry felt Sadie's body stiffen and then she stalked back to the camp bed and glared up at Kassandra. Slowly, never taking her eyes off the enforcer, Sadie leaned in and deliberately bit her on the ankle. Hard.

Kassandra cursed quietly as she went to hit the cat.

Sadie sprang on top of the camp bed and crouched low, muscles tense in her lithe body as a growl rumbled through her.

Kassandra lowered her hand and rubbed at her ankle. 'There was no need to bite me.'

Sadie swatted her arm and then once again jumped down and sauntered to the flap of the tent. Then she turned her head to stare back at Kassandra.

Kassandra gazed at her for a long and silent moment, fear flitting across her face. Then her shoulders slumped, and she huffed out a sigh. 'Fine. I'll come with you. But don't blame me if this ends up with Merry getting captured and locked up with the others.' As she stood to follow Sadie, Kassandra muttered, 'or dead.'

A chill went through Merry at the words, but she pushed her unease aside to concentrate on Sadie's exit from the camp, with Kassandra at her heels.

Sadie took a different route, heading for an area that was hidden by a stand of trees to the left of the camp. As they neared it, the cat's sensitive nose picked up the scent of human waste. While she didn't appreciate being linked and having that smell in her head, Merry admired the cat's foresight. To anyone watching, it would look as if Kassandra was visiting the latrines.

Mentally working to block the pungent aroma, Merry remained connected to Sadie as the cat led Kassandra on a winding route through the forest. Then the cat stopped a short distance from where Merry and the others waited and her connection with the familiar ceased.

Merry opened her eyes, head spinning at the change in view, and she took a moment to orient herself. Then she beckoned for the others to follow her as she moved through the trees to where Sadie had led Kassandra.

The enforcer held herself rigid as Merry entered the small clearing, though her eyes widened at the sight of Gabriel. 'Mage Fairweather, I did not expect to find you here.' Her eyes narrowed as she looked from him to Merry. 'Though perhaps I shouldn't be surprised. I heard about what happened at the Water focal point, and your fondness for Merry had been noted previously, though not as dramatically.'

Merry flushed, remembering the scorching kiss that had taken place when Gabriel had linked with her to share the combined might of all the magic users. There had been no time to discuss what had happened, their current mission leaving little time for heart-to-hearts. But she would never forget the way his presence had enveloped her, the admiration he held for her shining through the link. After they rescued the witches, there would be even less chance of finding the privacy needed to see if those feelings would lead further. That was probably not even an option, given her plan to return to her own world once she had made a new transportation spell.

She pushed those thoughts aside as Kassandra turned to face her.

'Karl was livid that you ruined his plan in Marshland, and even more so when he heard you recovered from magical exhaustion. He wants you dead, no matter how much Lord Andel claims you would be a valuable ally once he has bound you to his cause.' Kassandra's expression darkened. 'Make no mistake, if he finds out you are here he will do whatever it takes to see you dead. Even if it costs Andel the crown.'

Merry gulped at hearing it stated so plainly. The memory of being at his mercy within the depths of the Marshland Dam was another that would never leave her. Still, she lifted her chin and eyed Kassandra. 'I am not going to let fear of what might happen stop me from doing what is right. I am going to free those witches,' she said as she pointed in the direction of the prison, 'and you're going to help me.'

The colour leached from Kassandra's face. 'Are you insane? There are hundreds of militias guarding the prison. Not to mention those with magic. You wouldn't have a chance, even if I were stupid enough to help you. It's impossible.'

'You thought it would be impossible to destroy the poison stones in Marshland, but we did it.'

Kassandra scoffed. 'You needed the help of every Water witch or mage you could find in Marshland, and even then it nearly killed you. It can't be done.' She gave an angry shake and then heaved out a sigh. 'Well, if that is the only reason your familiar came to fetch me then we are done.' She made to walk off, but Gabriel stepped into her path, though his gaze was fixed on Merry.

Do we trust her not to run straight to her brother? Beethoven's mental tone was deeper than Sadie's.

Instead of answering, Merry stepped up and placed a hand on Kassandra's shoulder. 'If you tell Karl we are here, you're putting all of Tirana in danger and going against your oath to the guild. Or did Karl get his new pet to break it before Lord Andel sent him after me?'

Kassandra's eyes widened. 'What are you talking about?'

Merry gave her a brief description of the black-haired man with the subverted heartstones, leaving out Tara's name. 'With these heartstones, a Spirit mage can bind your oath without your consent. He's going to make all those witches swear to obey Karl and Lord Andel, and if you think you'll be spared then you don't know your brother as well as you think you do.'

The fresh pallor showed Kassandra knew exactly what fate awaited her once the black-haired stranger arrived with the heartstones.

Merry gave her plea one more shot. 'Help us free them, and we will make sure Karl can't touch you.'

As before, when Merry had suggested Kassandra come with them while escaping Marshland Dam, hope filled her eyes. But then fear settled into her gaze and she shook her head. 'I have to go back. He'll be expecting me to come and see him after Captain Baldwin reports.' She visibly hesitated before adding, 'I know you probably won't believe me, but I do hope you find a way to free them. No one should be made to serve against their will, and I promise I will not tell Karl that you are here. But whatever you are going to do you need to do it fast.' With that she headed off through the trees at a fast pace.

I will follow, to make sure she keeps her word. Sadie glanced back at Merry, before disappearing through the trees after Kassandra.

Merry, Gabriel, Ellen and Beethoven hurried back to their hidden vantage point at the outcrop and were in time to see Kassandra exit the tree-line and head straight for her brother's tent. Body tense, Merry waited for the outcry that would signal a betrayal. But there was no alarm or sign of mobilisation in the camp. It appeared Kassandra had kept her word.

Indeed. She has not spoken at all, and Karl appears to have little interest in his sister. Sadie once again shared her consciousness with Merry.

The familiar was crouched at the rear of the tent, her head poked under the canvas. From there she could see Karl sprawled out on a chaise lounge covered in velvet brocade, while Kassandra was sitting on a plain wooden chair at a small desk, using a feathered quill to write out a letter dictated to her by her brother. From the sounds of it, Lord Andel had promised to make Karl lord of Marshland once he was proclaimed king, and the former enforcer was angling for further rewards for his ongoing support.

Lady Beatrice would not be happy to have her province stripped from her family, but if Merry and the others could figure out how to free Britta and the rest of the witches that future would never come to pass.

She sent her senses ranging, but this time she looked beneath the prison.

The mountain range that sheltered the camp was pockmarked with caves. None allowed access through to Windemere, like the tunnel they had used to sneak into Andelmine, but some of them were of a good size. She scouted out the closest to the camp and a route to it that would keep them hidden.

When she was sure of the way forward, she

broached the idea with her friends. 'We can tunnel underground, into the centre of the camp.' With the tents all bunched up together, the guards should not be able to see what was happening in the centre. She hoped.

'That would take a lot of Earth magic, and what if they sense it?' Ellen waved a hand towards where the mages and witches were training.

'The flow of magic has been almost constant since we arrived, and only strong mages can sense when magic is being used nearby. It would be hard for them to pinpoint where it was coming from either way,' said Gabriel.

I will remain in the camp. Just because Kassandra has not betrayed you yet, does not mean she will continue to do so.

The longer you stay in their camp, the more chance you will be discovered. Merry's stomach knotted at the thought of what Karl might do if he caught Sadie.

I will flee at the first sign of danger. But it is important that we have eyes on the camp, in case of trouble.

With the cat's mind set, there was nothing for Merry to do but lead her other friends to the cave she had picked out. There she used her magic to dig into the hard ground, while Gabriel employed Air to shift the displaced earth into the back of the cave. With their magic disguised by the use of magic in the camp, they worked long into the afternoon, but only managed to make it halfway to the camp.

Each time they took a break, Ellen did what she

could to shore up their energy. After a quick snack, and a drink of magic water they would begin again.

Night had fallen and the sounds coming from both the prison and the militia camp had stilled. There was only the occasional noise and Sadie informed her most of the people were in their tents. The only ones still awake were the sentries on the outskirts and the guards in the four guard posts. Kassandra had retreated to her tent, and Karl was snoring on the chaise lounge in his.

Merry was careful to go slowly when she broke through the last section and made an opening in the ground in the middle of the prison tents. She used the last of the discarded soil to form rudimentary steps and used her magic to make them as solid as possible, ready to be used by dozens of witches to escape. With the night sky appearing above the hole she had made, Merry leaned against the wall of her tunnel and wiped sweat from her eyes. She was tired, but there was no time to waste.

Ellen appeared at her side and silently handed her the water bottle. Merry cleared the grit out of her mouth and took a deep swallow of the magically infused water. Then she brushed as much soil off her clothes and body as possible.

With Ellen's magic water tingling on her tongue and giving her renewed energy, she cautiously poked her head through the gap and could see no one about, her senses showing her all the captured witches were in their tents, presumably sleeping since it had to be near midnight. Merry clambered out of the hole and eyed the tents. She had no idea which one Britta would be in, and the sparks of colour were no help as she hadn't known how to 'see' what ability a person had when she'd met them before. She moved towards the nearest tent, and then gasped as shadowy figures burst out of the one beside it and quickly surrounded her.

Her heart thudded loudly in her chest; she was sure it was a trap.

The figures came closer, and the moon cast light on familiar features. Merry's heart resumed a more normal beat when Britta smiled at her. The leader of the witches made to speak, but Merry held up a hand for silence as she silently recited her invisibility spell in her head and spread it to encompass Britta and the others.

As soon as she was sure they would be safe from prying eyes and ears, Merry said, 'We need to get all of you out of here. Andel has someone coming with heart-stones. He can bind an oath to him without your consent.'

Britta gave a sharp nod and indicated to the ones with her to wake the rest of the witches. Then, as they were being gathered, she said to Merry, 'When an Earth witch told me there was something strange happening beneath our feet, I never expected it would be you. I thought you had your own quest to complete and no interest in helping us. Or have you finished your task?'

Merry shook her head. 'My quest is still ongoing, but

I came here as soon as I heard what was going to happen to you all.' She decided against mentioning that it was Tara who had convinced her to mount a rescue. Time enough to tell Britta her daughter had been one of the first to have their oath to obey Andel bound against her will. She did not look forward to that conversation at all.

The exodus from the prison camp went swiftly, with Merry stretching her spell as far as she could, wincing each time one of the witches made a noise as they were shown to the hole and ushered down the steps to freedom. Merry was tense, all her focus on making sure the guards in the posts did not realise their prisoners were escaping. She moved back with Britta and Gregor to let the last group of witches access the hole, her aching head looking forward to no longer having to hold the invisibility spell so wide. Soon there were only a few witches left aboveground, and none too soon as the shadows were beginning to lighten. Dawn was approaching, and once it grew light the guards would expect to see movement, becoming suspicious when no one appeared. The farther away they were when that happened the better.

Sadie had left the camp and was at the cave by the time the last witch started down the earthen steps. After him, there was only Merry, Britta and Gregor to go. The witch was halfway down when a discordant note sung in Merry's head.

It was as familiar as it was jarring.

The black-haired man had arrived at the gates to the prison, and he had the subverted heartstones with him.

Merry cast her senses out and could feel dozens of militias also at the gates, along with the red and white spark that was Karl and the more muted spark she associated with Kassandra.

Their time had run out.

CHAPTER 9

*M*erry urged Gregor to follow the last witch down the stairs, and for Britta to go next. She would go last, and once she was clear she would use the soil in the steps to form a roof over the opening. Her head was aching from holding her invisibility spell for so long, but she should have magic left to cover the hole she'd made and make it solid enough that people could walk on it. Without an obvious escape route, it should take Karl's magic users time to figure out how the witches escaped. That was time Merry and the others would use to get as far away from the prison as possible.

As she waited for her turn to descend, Merry worked to shore up the edges of the hole, coaxing the top soil to harden. From there she would form struts to jut into the centre of the gap to hold up the roof. Gregor reached the floor of the tunnel, and Britta was about to take the first step when a song filled Merry's head. It started softly, as it wrapped around her mind, gaining a foothold. Then it began to build in strength until it was all she could think about. The world ebbed away, the soil she had been working with falling over the lip of the hole without her magic to hold it up.

Britta stopped and turned to her with a quizzical look. 'Merry, what's wrong?'

The other woman's voice was faint, almost drowned out by the song spreading throughout every part of Merry's being, seeking to bend her to its will. Fear sent adrenaline rushing through Merry's body, and she used it to shut out the song. But it was so strong, so invasive, that it was like trying to cut away a part of herself. She could sense the man behind it, his smug satisfaction as his song strengthened in intensity, stopping her from calling out to Britta, even as he urged her to turn around and come to him.

Her body wanted to obey his call, but she clamped down on the response even as she frantically sought to free herself from his mental grasp. There had to be a way.

His song was so loud it reverberated within her head, and she wished she could place her hands over her ears to drown it out... not that it would do any good. Instead she tried to sing her own song, to counteract the effects of his.

At first, it had no effect, but she kept going, mentally humming the tune that had freed her from the lure of the heartstone back at the guild tower. Slowly, the song he sang began to lessen in volume, and she was able to hum her tune aloud. She soaked it up, letting it fill her body, using it to push out every trace of the siren song. Her muscles twitched and she was finally able to move her head.

The song grew louder, more insistent, but Merry was able to block it out as she faced Britta. 'Go. Now.' With a stumbling step, Merry lurched forward and pushed Britta down the next step. The witch quickly descended the makeshift steps, and Merry followed, her movements freeing up as she went. There was no point in covering the hole, now the element of surprise had been stripped away.

Instead, when Merry reached the bottom she hurried away from the steps and braced both hands on the walls of her tunnel. Then she drew on the strength of the Earth to collapse the ground around the hole, covering the steps and blocking the end of the tunnel. Dust and soil flew through the air, and she flung up a wall of air to protect herself until the rumble of earth ceased. With the wall of earth between her and the black-haired man, his song was muted, and she felt more herself. Voices called out from behind her, and she spun to find Britta and Gregor talking to Ellen and Gabriel. Merry took her staff and pack from Gabriel.

'We have to go. He's here with the heartstones.'

Alarm covered their faces but they quickly rallied and Merry hustled them down the tunnel. They had to get to the other end before Andel's forces discovered the cave they had used to get to the prison camp. They could be trapped in the tunnel, with no way of getting out. Merry was exhausted, the mental fight against the black-haired man's song taking the last of her energy. The thought of having to blast through metres of dirt to make another tunnel made her head pound. It had taken her hours to build this one, and that was without being attacked...

...or turned into a statue by some freaky song.

Shouts rang out through the tunnel and Merry feared they were going to be too late, but when she reached the exit into the cave she found all the witches there, milling about, fright in their voices and movements. She pushed through to the mouth of the cave along with Gabriel, Ellen, Britta and Gregor.

Sadie and Beethoven were waiting near the exit.

I'm sorry I didn't detect them until it was too late. They must have had someone powerful enough to create an invisibility spell like yours. They didn't drop the shield until they were at the camp.

Merry brushed aside Sadie's apology, though she dreaded the idea of facing a mage who could hide large groups as she did. She peeked outside the cave and could see no sign of Andel's forces, but that didn't mean they weren't there, given Sadie's information. They couldn't go back towards the tunnel she and her friends had used to sneak into Andelmine. That would take far too long, and it would lead them closer to the camp. Yet they couldn't stay where they were.

Merry ushered everyone out of the cave, getting them to head along the base of the mountain range. There was no point using her invisibility spell to hide them. With so many people, their tracks would give them away and she had to conserve what strength she had left. Pain thudding through her head with each step, she raced to the front of the group, scanning the mountain with her Earth senses in hope of finding another way through. There were plenty of abandoned mineshafts they could hide in but to do so would only trap them, unless she was able to find a way out.

One of the mines a short distance ahead went deeper into the mountain than the others. Merry stretched her senses as far as they would go but couldn't reach the other end of the mine or the other side of the mountain. This could be their best shot.

A cry went up behind her and then Merry felt a flash of heat in her solar plexus, so hot it made her entire body flush. Seconds later a fireball hit the trees to the left of where she stood. There was no time to find another way. Not if the enemy was throwing fireballs at them.

She spun and grabbed the arm of the witch behind her, this woman wearing a dirty purple dress. 'There is a mineshaft just ahead.' She envisioned the opening she had seen and did her best to mentally share it with the witch.

'I see it.'

'Lead the others there. I'll buy you time.'

The witch gave a determined nod and then ushered her companions forward, while Merry ran in the opposite direction, back towards where the fireball had come from.

Another flare of heat signalled the launching of another fireball, and this time she sensed the gust of Air that diverted its path to land in the trees to the side. The flames from the first fireball were already burning the forest, this one adding to the smoke, heat and haze, as well as the distress of the fleeing witches. Merry called for them to hurry, to follow the leader to safety.

Then she rounded a curve in the mountain and found Gabriel, Ellen, Britta and Gregor facing off against a Fire mage and over a dozen militia. A handful of Air witches had remained with them, and Gabriel had them all linking hands behind him. He was using their power to bolster his own as he sought to stop the fireballs from reaching them.

'The others are closing in,' yelled Britta as soon as she spotted Merry. 'We won't be able to hold them off for long.'

Merry didn't spare time in responding. Ignoring the tiredness in her body and mind, she dug deep into the side of the mountain in front of the Fire mage with her Earth magic and wrenched it sideways, creating a cascading river of rocks and dirt that momentarily blocked them from sight. She stumbled, exhaustion threatening to drop her where she stood. But she forced it down, wiping sweat and grit from her face as she reached for her friends.

'Let's go,' she said, tugging Gabriel's arm to pull him around.

He shook his head, stumbling as he broke the link with the Air witches, but he quickly rallied.

With Ellen and the others at their back, they raced side by side for the entrance to the mine. The flames in the forest to the side of them had intensified, and the air was thick with smoke but neither she nor Gabriel spared any effort to clear it away. There was no time.

They reached the mineshaft and Merry gripped her staff, commanding it to light as they ran into the dark depths in search of the others. There were smaller tunnels branching off from the main one, but Merry had shown the Spirit witch the path through the centre of the mountain and she could sense the other woman had stayed true to the path and that the others had followed her. The tunnel they were in was wide enough that she had Gabriel on one side of her and Ellen on the other. Sadie and Beethoven streaked ahead of them, while Britta and Gregor, with the remaining witches were just behind.

It was dark and claustrophobic in the tunnel, more so than the first one they had used. Maybe it was that they were being chased and she knew there was no exit at the end. Either way, they had to keep going. She kept her senses ranging ahead, feeling through the rock to find the thinnest sections between caves.

There.

A large cavern was up ahead, just in front of the main group, one that would lead them to safety. But how to signal to the witches that had already gone ahead, led by the Spirit witch? She may have been able to impart the path, but telepathy was beyond her skills.

'Are any of you Spirit witches?' Merry called over her shoulder, her voice a wheeze from her exertions.

'I am,' said Britta, her voice just as strained as Merry's.

'Can you tell those ahead of us who have an ability with Spirit that they need to stop?'

There was no answer for a moment, and Merry glanced back to see that Britta had her eyes closed while being led along by Gregor.

Then Britta opened her eyes. 'Done.'

A loud clatter came from behind Britta and Merry turned back to the front, striving to increase her speed. She didn't need to scan behind them to know their pursuers had found the mine entrance.

They caught up with the rest of their group and Merry shared a relieved smile with Gabriel as she pushed through the crowd to place one hand on the side of the tunnel, while the other held her heartstone pressed against her staff. 'If any of you are Earth witches, be ready to shore up the roof. I'm breaking us out of here.' She hoped so, anyway. She could feel the trembling in her body, her hands shaking, from working so much magic. She was risking magical exhaustion, and there were no guild mages nearby to heal her.

But she didn't have a choice. The fate that awaited them if they didn't escape was worse than burning out her magic and ending up dead or in a coma. She would not let Karl get his hands on her or allow the black-haired man to take over her body with his siren song.

With time running out, there was no finesse to her mental touch as Merry drove her senses into the rock face. She wormed her way through minute gaps in the rock, expanding them, trusting that Ellen would lead the others in making sure the roof of the mine tunnel did not come down on their heads, at least not yet.

Sweat coated her body and stung her eyes, but Merry did not lift her hand or stop what she was doing. Soon a loud crack drowned out all other sounds as a section of the wall split open, tumbling to the ground within the tunnel in a cascade that sent rock chips and dirt flying through the air. But none of it hit Merry, thanks to a barricade of Air that resonated with the familiar taste of Gabriel's magic.

The barricade then became a ram, pushing aside the rocks that had fallen to block the exit Merry had created, clearing a path for the witches to scramble through.

Ellen and several witches stood with their hands poised against the rock wall beside Merry's gap, and she sensed them straining to keep the rock ceiling from tumbling down. When everyone else was out, Merry took over the task of holding up the roof and then ushered them all out. She was the last to slip through, wide eyed as the Fire mage and several militias came into view down the tunnel.

She hesitated to release her magic. Could she risk entombing these people in the mine forever?

But if she didn't, they would swiftly overtake her group and it would all be for nothing.

She felt a warm presence at her side and Gabriel placed his hand over hers. Then he tugged her back through the gap as the ceiling collapsed in the mine.

The witches they'd rescued were huddled in the centre of the cavern; relief tempered with fear on many of their faces. They were a lot cleaner and looked better fed than the ones Andel had imprisoned in his dungeon. With his new batch of heartstones and the man who could bind oaths on the unwilling, there had been no need to starve them into submission.

Britta and Gregor were nearby, watching Merry and Gabriel with wary expressions. She could tell they both knew the rescue was not successful yet. Andel had Earth witches and mages. He would be able to clear her blockade. They had to keep going. Merry made to move off, but Ellen stepped into her path.

'You're not going anywhere until I heal you,' she said, holding out a water skin.

Begrudging the time, even though she knew it was necessary, Merry gulped down the magically infused water while Ellen did her best to heal some of the exhaustion racking her body. Then, with fresh energy flooding through her, she ushered everyone to the exit from the cavern that she had detected earlier. It was narrow, meaning they had to go single file and she chafed at the delay, sure their enemies would be making the most of it. It felt as if an eternity had passed before they all were outside in the chilly morning air. More than a few of the witches were not dressed for the cold and would need shelter soon. Despite being better fed than before, they had still been cooped up for days and were out of condition. They would not be able to travel far or fast.

They ran into the forest as a loud crack came from within the cavern behind them, followed by an avalanche of rocks. Merry hurried her charges along as fast as they could go, though having to wind their way through trees wasn't helping. She sought a clearer path and steered them in that direction.

Heat flashed through her body, and she shouted a warning a split second before the whoosh of a fireball swept overhead and hit the trees in front of her.

She veered to the right even as another fireball slammed into the tops of the trees in that direction. That left them only one direction to go. Cries of fear mixed with ones of pain as shrapnel from the exploded trees filled the air. The heat was intense as the flames quickly devoured the trees and then moved on to the next ones. Soon there was a raging fire on either side of

Merry and her group. Smoke stung her eyes and heat made the air hazy as they blindly ran in the only direction that was safe.

They got ahead of the fire and Merry led them into a gap between the trees. As they fled into what appeared to be a cut through in another mountain range the crackle of flames chased them. Too late Merry released they had been chased into a blind canyon. It narrowed to a point, giving them nowhere to run, while the fire raging at their backs cut off any chance of retreat.

This was madness.

Surely Andel did not seek to slaughter all the witches he had captured? There had to be a way to extinguish the flames.

Shouts and the sound of fighting came from behind her and Merry spun around and pushed her way through the frightened witches to find a bunch of Andel's forces at the end of the canyon.

Gabriel, Gregor and a dozen witches were using magic to keep them back but there was too many of them. Merry wanted to help, but their forces were tangled, making it hard to tell who was friend and who was foe. The only one that stood out was the Fire Mage. Hate was etched on his face, as he prepared to throw a fireball at Gabriel.

As before, there was the flash of heat in Merry's solar plexus and she focused on it, trying to find a way to extinguish the flames. But though the heat inside her intensified, it had no effect on the fire ball, It arced in the air, heading straight for Gabriel and Gregor, who had their backs turned as they fought an Air mage and a group of militias from Greystone.

Merry called out, but with the battle ongoing her voice was drowned. She had to do something. She whipped up wind, sending it to batter at the fireball, to deflect its course.

It careered in the air and landed to the side of the canyon, immediately engulfing the trees that stood there.

The Fire mage spun around as the flames blocked half the exit. He called out a retreat. The flames whipped across the opening as the Fire mage did something to hold them back long enough for the bulk of his forces to slip through the gap. One figure in a red robe ran in the other direction, towards Merry's friends, just as the Fire mage let the fire go so that the exit was completely blocked.

Merry's group ran further into the dead-end canyon as the fire raged towards them. There was no escape. They would be incinerated if she didn't do something soon. There was no water here to call on, and the fire was too immense to be pushed back by wind. In desperation, Merry reached into the walls of the canyon and commanded them to fall, smothering the flames.

When the dust settled, there were spot fires, but Gregor rallied some of the others to put them out, leaving them trapped in a fire ravaged canyon with no way out. A pained cry came from behind Merry, and she turned to see two witches holding up a struggling figure in an ash coated red robe.

Brown hair tangled and face covered in dirt, Kassandra glared at the men holding her arms.

'Let me go, you imbeciles, or I'll bash your heads against that rock.' She indicated with her head to the side where a large rock hovered in the air.

One of the men holding her stiffened, giving her a shake. But the other, wearing a green tunic, reached out his free hand and touched her on the forehead. Immediately, Kassandra's eyes rolled back, and she went limp in their arms.

Merry was numb, exhausted, and she slumped to the ground before her knees could collapse under her. She could sense the fire still raging in the forest on the other side of the canyon, the Fire mage desperate to hold it back long enough for his forces to escape.

There would be no attempt to recapture them—at least until the fire had burned itself out or Andel found a way to extinguish it. But for them there was no need to hurry. Merry might have put out the fire on their side but in doing so she had completely closed off the exit, meaning they were now trapped in a canyon with sheer sides.

She was too tired to care that they were sitting ducks, and from the groans and mutters coming from those around her most of the witches felt the same. Witches in green tunics and dresses moved through them, healing those that needed it, Merry got up and moved over to where Kassandra had been laid on the ground. Someone had taken the time to remove her red robe and wadded it up under her head as a makeshift pillow.

She looked different, unconscious; the tension gone from her face. Kassandra wasn't the only member of Andel's forces lying in the shadow cast by the canyon wall. Most of them wore militia uniforms, but two were witches. There was no way for her to tell if they had been willing members of Andel's forces or victims. But she got to her feet and signalled for Ellen to join her.

'Can you wake her up?' She pointed at Kassandra.

'Sure. What about them?' Ellen looked at the two witches, one a Water witch and the other an Air witch.

Merry shook her head. 'We need to know if they are enslaved or not. Kassandra can tell us.'

Gabriel came over to them. 'Do you think that's a good idea? She said she won't betray her brother.'

Merry explained what she had seen. 'She had the chance to leave with the others. Instead she stayed. She may not want to betray Karl, but she knows what he's doing is wrong.' Merry thought about the fear in Kassandra's eyes when she was around her brother. 'I think this was a cry for help.' She waved at where Ellen was using her magic to gently wake Kassandra.

Without the red robe covering her simple black dress, Kassandra looked younger, vulnerable, as her eyelids fluttered before opening. Her expression was dazed, eyes unfocused as Ellen helped her to sit up.

Then fear sharpened her features as the reality of her situation hit.

She narrowed her eyes as she scanned the canyon before fixing her gaze on Merry.

'I hope you have a plan to get us out of this mess, because Karl will hit us with everything he has. He does not like to lose.'

Merry raised an eyebrow. 'Us?' Just because she thought Kassandra was searching for a way out didn't mean she was going to trust her completely. She needed a commitment from the enforcer before they could take the next step.

Kassandra didn't look away, though she took a shuddering breath before simply stating, 'Us.'

*T*here was no time to rest or to test if Kassandra's decision to throw her lot in with Merry and the others was genuine or not. With time running out, they had to find a way out of the dead-end canyon before Karl and his army found a way through the blockage Merry had caused. They needed a way that did not involve her using any magic. Her head pounded, her limbs felt like jelly, and moving made her stomach queasy. Even with Ellen giving her more of the magically infused water and healing the worst of her aches and pains, the thought of using her magic made Merry wince.

Luckily for her, Gabriel quickly came up with a plan.

Merry sat on the ground with her back against a rock, with Sadie on her lap. Petting the cat's silky black fur was soothing, the soft rumble of the familiar's purr easing the tension in her body that had built during the escape. Kassandra sat beside her, while Gregor and a couple of other strong witches of all abilities acted as guards for the enforcer. On the opposite side of the canyon, Gabriel directed all the Earth witches to use their magic to carve foot and handholds in the sheer wall farthest away from where they had entered. From what she could see, Ellen was proving the most adept at the task, even giving advice to some of the other witches.

For a woman who claimed that she wasn't a strong witch, Merry's friend had proved time and again how dedicated and resourceful she was. Yes, her heartstone would aid her, but it was an innate part of Ellen that had her give one hundred and ten percent on any task. Merry was thankful the healer was the person who had found her grandmother's broken spell box, and that her care and concern for others and need to do the right thing had led to Ellen joining her and Sadie on their quest to remake the transportation spell.

She shuddered to think what would have happened to her if she had not found such a wonderful and courageous friend. For sure, she would never have made it out of Dryton. Instead she would have been imprisoned by the guild, never getting the chance to learn about her magic that now felt like a part of her.

While they waited for the handholds to be created, the rest of the witches bustled around the canyon floor under Britta's direction, sorting the meagre belongings they had fled with into piles. They were using items of clothing to create makeshift packs as climbing the canyon wall, even with handholds, would not be an easy task. Those who were stronger and more agile were tasked with carrying the packs.

Ellen and Merry had given Britta every scrap of food and water they had, to share among the witches. It had barely amounted to a mouthful each. They would have to find supplies, fast, if they were to survive the trek through Windemere's province to Dryton.

Not that Merry had divulged their destination to Britta as yet. First she had to summon the courage to tell her what had happened to Tara. With a sigh, she asked Sadie to hop off her lap and then scrambled to her feet. Kassandra made to follow her, but a warning from Gregor had her subsiding, though the sour expression on the enforcer's face meant she was not happy about it.

Tough. Merry had no intention of discussing her plan with Karl's sister in earshot.

She reached Britta's side in moments, catching the older woman's attention, and together they moved to stand in the shade of the canyon wall. After making sure no one was listening nearby, Merry took a deep breath and began her sorry tale.

'I met Tara, while I was imprisoned by the guild. She helped me escape, but not by her choice.' In a low voice, she explained what had happened, unable to miss the pain in Britta's eyes as she listened intently.

When she finished talking, Britta was silent for a moment, head downcast. Then she looked up and met

Merry's gaze, hers fierce and determined. 'I will go to the tower and find a way to break her of this oath. There has to be a way to free her.'

'I've been thinking about that, about the man who bound Tara's oath. He has Singer blood. I've met the Mistress of Songs, and I'm sure she would be horrified to find out what has happened. If anyone can break the oath, it would be her.'

'Then we go there, after we free Tara, and get her to break the oath.'

Merry shook her head. 'I can't help Tara, not yet, and the Singers have closed off their mountain. You could go there and try to find a way in, to get them to help you, but because of what Lord Andel did they have cut all contact with the rest of Tirana. I doubt they would make an exception for you. But I helped them, and I believe they will listen to me. First though, I need to get a Fire charm, from the focal point in Seahaven Province. Then I will return to the guild tower and free your daughter.' As well as get her Spirit stone, of course.

Britta narrowed her eyes, nostrils flaring. 'You expect me to just sit back and do nothing? She's my daughter.'

'I know. But she is safest where she is. If she leaves the tower, Andel could order her to use her magic against you and she would have to obey. She was devastated that she was forced to betray me and Gabriel. What do you think it would do to her if she was made to hurt you, or worse?'

Denial flared in Britta's eyes but Merry could also

see doubt. She drove home her point. 'You have seen what happened to those witches who didn't escape Andel's dungeon unscathed. Do you want that to happen to Tara?'

Britta shook her head, but when she went to speak Merry cut her off. 'Andel is not the only threat facing Tirana. I need your help, yours and the rest of the witches we rescued, to stop witch hunters gaining access to a portal and coming here from my world to continue their persecution of those with magic.' She explained about the waning wards and how *Huntingdon Inc.*, a front for the witch hunters, had been trying to find a way to Tirana for generations.

'If I don't go back, and renew the wards my grand-mother set, they will be able to break through. Sadie tells me they have witches in their employment, the descendants of witches they enslaved centuries ago. They will come here, and they will find Tirana in turmoil, thanks to Lord Andel, and they will not hesitate to strike. We have to prevent that from happening.'

Britta straightened up and eyed Merry. 'You really think they will come here, these witch hunters?'

Merry thought about the history of the witch hunts back home, the way many people suspected of being a witch had been burned at the stake. The witch hunts were the reason her and Britta's ancestors had fled to Tirana. That had been hundreds of years ago, and the world was supposedly a more civilised and enlightened place now. But Merry knew there were always fanatics determined to follow the hateful teachings of others to sow death and destruction. The news reports back home were full of such acts.

'Yes, they will come, and they will destroy every witch they can.'

Britta was silent for a long moment, and then she gave a sigh. 'What do you need from me?'

Relief swamped Merry at Britta's question, the feeling of one fewer thing to worry about giving her a calm that had been missing ever since she arrived in Tirana. 'The portal is near Dryton, in Rangaleemore Province. Once we get out of here, we will head to Dryton. I need you and the others to set up camp near the portal, to be ready in case I fail. The witch hunters cannot be allowed to gain a foothold here, and you are the only person I trust to see this through. As soon as I get the last two charms, I will join you and reset the wards. Then, when Tirana is safe, from witch hunters at least, we will free Tara from the guild tower and get the Singers to break the oath.'

Britta gave a nod, though her expression was troubled as she re-joined her peers.

Merry didn't blame her for being concerned. It was easy enough to say what she planned to do, but to achieve Tara's freedom they would have to surmount numerous obstacles, not least of which was Ophelia Fairweather and the guild.

She would worry about that when the time came.

The first group of witches had begun the ascent of

the cliff. Gabriel stood at the base, ready with his magic to use wind as a cushion should any of them slip. Other Air witches stood nearby to bolster him if needed.

When it was Merry's turn to climb, she wiped sweaty palms on her dress as she stepped forward and placed her right foot in the first of the footholds. Her staff was secured to her back, and Sadie rested in a makeshift sling alongside it. Merry also carried the spell box containing the charms she had collected so far, determined not to be parted from it.

Conscious of Gabriel's confident gaze, and with Ellen ready to climb alongside her, she reached for the first handhold and pulled herself up. Then she reached for the next one, slowly climbing her way up the canyon wall, determined not to stop or look down. Even with Gabriel below, ready to catch her if she fell, Merry did not feel safe. The side of the canyon was at least four storeys high. It was a small comfort to know that over half of their party had successfully scaled it, with only a few minor slips that Gabriel and the Air witches had taken care of easily.

It was one thing to watch others climb a rock face without a safety harness; another to actually do it herself. Having Sadie on her back messed with her centre of gravity, though the familiar remained still throughout the process, her mental voice also quiet. After what felt like hours, Merry eventually pulled herself to the top and gratefully accepted the helping hands that tugged her away from the edge. Her arms and legs trembled from the climb, and she sank onto her knees in the thick grass, removing Sadie's sling and placing it on the ground in front of her as Ellen joined her.

'Let's never do that again,' said her friend, face gleaming with sweat and her eyes wide.

As Sadie clambered out of the sling and gave her lithe body a shake, the little cat wholeheartedly agreed.

The sun shone down on the exposed point they were now on, though there was a chill wind blowing. Most of the witches who had already climbed to the top had moved to the edge of the nearby forest. Merry waited for Gabriel and Beethoven, the last to scale the cliff. She got as close to the edge as she could, ready with her Air magic in case he slipped. But Gabriel did not falter, and he and his familiar were soon standing beside her.

'Are you feeling okay?' Gabriel moved closer, placing a hand on Merry's arm. 'Not feeling any ill effects from expending so much magic?'

Warmth flooded Merry's body, both from the level of concern he showed for her wellbeing and his nearness. Even after everything they had been through, he looked and smelled amazing, while she was sure she looked like a mess. She couldn't remember the last time she'd had a proper shower and been able to wash her hair. Every inch of her was covered in dirt from carving out the tunnel, some of it having burrowed in under her dress. She was in no condition to explore the emotions present in his clear gaze.

Cheeks flushing, she gave a quick nod. 'I'm fine. I'll be even better once we get as far away from here as possible.' She stepped back, indicating for Gabriel to walk beside her, and together they hurried to catch up to the others.

Tirana may have been a small country compared to Australia, but it didn't feel that small as she trekked along beside him. The group foraged for food as they went, making do with what berries, nuts and other edible plants they could find. But it was not enough to give them more than a mouthful of each. A dull ache settled into Merry's stomach, and her throat was dry from not enough water. But she did not complain. They were all in the same position. All they could do was continue to put one foot in front of the other until nightfall.

The experienced hunters among them had managed to capture a number of small animals to cook up when they stopped for the night, and Gregor beckoned Merry over when it was time to light the campfire.

'Britta tells me you need practice with Fire magic. What level are you at?'

Merry stared at him. 'Ah, I didn't know there were levels. I do most of my magic by instinct.'

He gave her a penetrating look. 'Instinct is a fine start, but we need to build on that so you can achieve true mastery over your element. What magic have you been able to do so far?' He waved a hand towards the cook fire and a small stream shot up in the air, and then danced above his open palm to form the shape of a bird in flight. 'Can you shape the flame?'

Merry grimaced. 'I can't do anything. The only elements I've been able to use so far are Earth, Water and Air.'

The flame above Gregor's hand disappeared in a puff of smoke. 'You haven't even conjured a single flame? What about controlling the flow of a fire? I saw you as we escaped, you pushed the fire back.'

'I used Air, not Fire.'

Gregor stared at her; brows lowered. 'So you haven't even had the first step, contact with Fire.'

Merry shrugged. She had felt something, a stirring in her stomach, when she had tried to connect with the fire. But it had not responded at all. 'Sorry. I'm new to all of this.' She waved a hand around the camp, taking in the assembled witches as they made the best of the situation, some using their elements to make the camp as safe as possible, while ones like Ellen tended to those who had been injured during their escape.

Gregor's hand shot out and he gripped her arm, pulling her forward.

'Hey, what are you doing?'

Gregor ignored her as he spun her around and then he shoved her outstretched hand into the fire.

Heat flared through Merry's fingers, instantly followed by searing pain. She shrieked, and tried to pull away, but Gregor's grip on her was too tight.

The heat intensified, and the pain became unbearable. A rolling wave swept over her body as she sought to break free, to escape the fire. To make it stop.

The fire vanished, only smoke remaining.

Gregor released Merry, and she fell backwards, clutching her burned hand in shock. Only, it wasn't burned at all. The fingers were just as they always were, only shaking. The pain was gone too.

She was dimly aware of Gabriel and Ellen saying something to Gregor, their voices raised, but she couldn't tear her eyes away from her hand. It should be burned to a crisp, mangled and melted after being held in the fire for so long. She should be writhing in agony. But other than the aches from trying to break Gregor's hold, she and her hand were fine.

She dragged herself to her feet, and poked Gregor in the back, making him swing around to face her. Despite the harsh words she could hear her friends saying to him, Gregor was relaxed and gave her a big smile.

'Well?' He raised his eyebrows.

'Why am I not burned?' She waved her hand in front of him. 'What the hell did you do to me?'

He raised his hands in front of his chest. 'I didn't do anything. You did it. You commanded the fire to stop burning and it obeyed. Now that you've had your catalyst moment, we can start your training.'

'My catalyst moment?'

'You said it yourself, your magic works on instinct. I figured, if you did have an affinity to Fire, then if I put you in a position where Fire was a threat your instincts would manifest in such a way to use the ability. I was right. It worked.'

Merry shook her head. 'But the pain, the heat. I felt the fire burning me.'

'That was your brain, telling you what it expected to feel. For anyone with a Fire affinity, they would not be seriously harmed, unless their affinity was so weak as to be almost non-existent. But from the ease with which you extinguished the fire, I would say you will have mage strength once you are fully trained.'

Merry narrowed her eyes. 'What if it didn't work? What if I didn't have an affinity with Fire at all?'

Gregor shrugged. 'Then you would have burned. But I was ready to extinguish the flames if that were the case, and your friend here is a capable healer. The damage would have been minimal.'

'You had no right to put Merry in danger.' Gabriel squared off against Gregor. 'She could have been seriously injured.'

Gregor shrugged again, not looking at all put out by Gabriel's anger. 'This method has been used to unleash magic in many a young apprentice who is reluctant to use their ability. There was no time to coddle the girl. She needs full access to her Fire magic if she is to have any chance of getting a Fire charm. Now the flame burns inside her, Merry has a chance she did not have before.'

Gregor was right. Merry did feel a flame burning inside her. It was different to what she felt from her other elemental affinities. He was also right about there being no time to waste. His methods might be extreme, but it had worked.

She turned to Gabriel. 'I'm fine.'

'You could have been seriously injured.'

'Yes, but I wasn't. I need to learn this stuff.'

He gave a reluctant nod, and Merry turned to Gregor. 'Show me what to do.'

Gregor was a hard taskmaster, but by the time Merry went to sleep on a pile of grass that had been enhanced by the Earth witches to be springy like a mattress, she was able to separate one flame from the fire and hold it in her palm without being burned. After tramping through the forest the following day, the next night was a repeat of her lessons. By the time she tumbled onto her grass mattress, Merry was able to get her chosen flame to form simple shapes. She was a long way from Gregor's skill level, but she was learning fast.

But would it be fast enough?

She had no idea what awaited her at the Fire focal point, but she doubted it would involve forming a fire bird or flower. Still, she was at least connected to the Fire element now. She might not be able to extinguish a fireball thrown at her by a Fire mage, but with the use of her combined elements she hoped she would be able to complete the task and get her next charm.

After another full day of travelling, they reached the outskirts of Dryton. Ellen directed most of the weary witches to her family's farm, giving them a letter of introduction that would urge her parents to take them in.

Merry stood beside her friend as the party set off. 'Do you think your parents would turn them away?'

Ellen shook her head. 'Not a chance. I'm more worried about how they will cope with so many new mouths to feed. Our farm is small. It barely produced enough to feed us, which is why I sold herbal remedies to make up the difference.'

Merry waved a hand at the retreating witches. 'All five elements are covered in that group, and none of them are freeloaders. Together they will be able to come up with a way to ensure the farm can provide for all of them.'

Ellen gave her a grateful smile. 'You're right. I just wish I could have gone with them, to explain everything to my mother and father. There was only so much I could put in a letter.'

A pang hit Merry, reminding her of how long it had been since she had seen her own parents. The last time not being a good one either. Ellen was clearly close to her mum and dad but getting caught up in Merry's quest had dragged her away from them and got her in trouble with the guild. As much as she didn't want to lose her friend, she couldn't keep Ellen by her side when her family needed her.

'You could go with them. Your parents would be happy to see you, and I'm sure they could do with your help.'

Ellen turned to face her, a smile on her face as she placed a hand on Merry's arm. 'Thank you. But I'm the strongest healer you've got. You need me.'

'I don't want you to come with me if you need to be with your family. Besides, it's dangerous.'

Ellen's face darkened. 'It's dangerous everywhere. It will be even more dangerous if we don't stop those witch hunters. I'm coming with you.'

Merry gave her friend a quick hug, relieved they would not be parted. Then they strode over to where Gabriel waited with Britta and the rest of the witches who would help her guard the portal.

Sadie took the lead from there, as Merry only had a vague idea of which direction to go. Soon they were all standing in the small clearing where she had entered Tirana. A tingle swept over her body as she drew closer to the very spot she'd landed in, the power of the portal thrumming through her now she was more attuned to the magic that created it. She was so close to home, and yet without a transportation spell she might have been a world away.

Gabriel stepped up beside her. 'Wishing you could go home?'

Merry gave him a small smile. 'A little. But that won't be happening anytime soon. Not until I have a Fire and Spirit charm.' She grimaced at the thought she had been so close to the Spirit focal point but blocked from getting the charm she needed by Lord Andel's people. If she'd been able to get it as they fled the tower, she would now need only one charm.

But she pushed the frustration down and focused on the now.

Britta was surveying the area. 'We will make our camp over there,' she said as she pointed to the left of the clearing. 'That way we will not be in direct sight if anyone does attempt to come through the portal, or easy targets if someone else comes looking for us.'

'Good idea,' said Merry. While the witch hunters were one concern, they could not forget that Andel was after them, and the guild would not be friendly towards them either. 'Do you have everything you need?' They'd been able to forage some supplies, and Ellen had given them the key to her shop to get more.

'We will be fine. We can contact the others if there is anything we need. We'll also set up lookouts around Dryton, to warn of anyone coming this way. You do your part, and then get back here as quick as you can so we can go to the tower to free my daughter and get your final charm.'

Confident that Britta had everything under control, Merry and her friends, and Kassandra, set off for Seahaven Province and the Fire focal point.

CHAPTER 11

*I*t was another two days march before they reached Seahaven Province, and a further day after that before they drew near the coast. They had travelled through the forest for as much of the journey as they could to avoid being seen by inhabitants of the towns they passed, not wanting to give anyone a chance to spot them and reveal that information to those who hunted them. Though there had been no sign of either Andel's forces or of the guild, Merry and her friends were sure they were out there.

Each night, Merry sat by the small campfire and manipulated the flames into shapes. Without Gregor to guide her, that was all she could accomplish. But at least she no longer had to shove her hand into the flames to trigger her elemental ability. She hoped her instincts would kick in to help her solve whatever challenge awaited her at the Fire focal point, to get her next charm, sure it wouldn't be something as easy as making shapes.

According to Gabriel and Sadie, the Fire focal point was in a grotto, inside a dormant volcano situated beside the harbour town of Haven, the largest town in Seahaven.

'Building a town next to a volcano is a bold choice, even if it is dormant,' said Merry. There were so many times volcanoes had caused death and destruction in her world, she wouldn't be comfortable living so close to one.

Gabriel chuckled. 'Actually, this is probably the safest place in Tirana. There is a school for Fire mages in Haven, with fourth year apprentices fine tuning the power of their element at the focal point. If there was even a chance the volcano was going to erupt, the mages and their apprentices would be able to neutralise the threat.'

'I agree with Merry,' said Kassandra, her mouth twisted in a bitter smile. 'Mages may think they could control an eruption, but pride can lead to the downfall of even the most powerful, and this volcano is home to an elemental focal point.'

Merry raised an eyebrow at the enforcer's words. Kassandra had been quiet for most of the journey, seeming to have accepted her role as prisoner even though there were no ropes or magical bindings to keep her with them. Until now, she had only talked when asked a direct question. She also never attempted to use her enforcer abilities to escape or to hinder them, though they continued to keep a close watch on her just in case.

Kassandra is right. Just because Mount Ashton has been dormant since your ancestors arrived in Tirana doesn't mean it won't erupt at some time in the future, and I fear even the strongest of Fire mages would be hard pressed to stop it.

'What about if the Fire mages linked, like we did at the Water focal point?' Merry asked, after explaining what Sadie had said to the others.

Gabriel gave a nod. 'I believe, with the combined efforts of the Fire mages and their apprentices, they would be able to contain it.'

'Well, let's hope that never happens,' said Ellen. 'Merry nearly died fighting the poisoned aquamarine in Marshland, even with the help of Water mages and witches. If something like that were to happen at the Fire focal point, it would be catastrophic.'

Merry shuddered at the thought of something like a poison stone inside a volcano. She turned to Kassandra. 'Lord Andel and your brother wouldn't go that far, would they?' But even as she asked the question, she knew anything was possible when it came to the deranged enforcer and the lord who wanted to be king.

'They never mentioned anything of that nature in my hearing, but I was not privy to their planning after I helped you escape the dam. Karl said he would not trust me until I was oath bound to obey him and Lord Andel.'

Her voice faltered on her last words, face pale and drawn as she turned to Merry.

'Do you really think you will find a way to break the oaths made by this Singer? I know some of the Spirit mages have been able to break existing oaths with heart-stones, when mages switched sides, but you're talking about something different, aren't you? Or do you have a stash of good heartstones somewhere and a Spirit mage strong enough?'

Merry stared back at Kassandra, debating what to tell her. Merry had noticed the enforcer listening intently anytime she and her friends talked about the black-haired man and how he could make people swear oaths against their will. Other than guessing he had Singer blood, as Merry did, they were no closer to understanding how it was possible. They had been careful not to mention in Kassandra's hearing that Merry's plan was to approach Alicia, Mistress of Songs for the Singers, to see if she was able to break the oaths that had been unwillingly bound.

For now, Merry settled with saying, 'The man who is working for Andel and your brother can do it, so I'm sure we can figure it out too.'

Kassandra's eyes narrowed. 'You'd better hope so. Because if my brother gets hold of you, and you can't break the oaths, you will be destroyed.'

Merry grimaced, well able to imagine Karl taking out his frustration on her once again. He would not let her live a second time. But she was spared having to answer

Kassandra when Sadie sent her a warning. She waved for her friends, and the enforcer, to be silent. Gabriel was already on alert, no doubt informed by Beethoven that something was wrong. As quietly as they could, the small group followed Sadie as she led them to a spot where they could look out on the road without being seen.

The road was full of people, many of them on foot, lugging large packs on their backs, while some had horses and carts laden with people and goods. Their shoulders were hunched forward, features drawn, dust from the road covering their faces and clothes. None of them were talking, an air of fear and concern rising from them, and all of them were heading in the opposite direction to Merry and her friends.

As she watched, a young man peeled away from the main group and headed into the trees near where she and the others crouched. Merry remained silent, hidden, until the man reached a spot right near her and set down his pack. Then he began to untie the laces holding his trousers up. Realising what he was about to do, and that she was in the firing line, she scrambled backwards, stepping on a twig as she ducked behind a large bush. She peered over the top to see if she had been spotted.

The man's eyes were wide, and he clutched at the waistband of his trousers as he peered into the trees. 'Is someone there?'

Merry was about to speak up, but Gabriel waved her back and then stepped forward. 'Forgive me, friend, I did not mean to startle you,' he said as he stepped out from behind a tree and approached the young man. 'I'm camped nearby and came to see what all the noise was.' He waved a hand back towards the road and the travellers on it.

The man's eyes narrowed. 'Are you a bandit, come to fleece me of what little possessions I have left?'

Gabriel shook his head, tone mild as he said, 'I assure you; I have no interest in your belongings. I merely seek information.'

The young man stared silently at Gabriel for a moment. Then he asked, 'What kind of information?'

'I wish to know why you and the others are heading inland. Have you been troubled by bandits?'

The man shook his head. 'There has been some trouble, but that is not why we flee. Mount Ashton is close to erupting.'

Gabriel gasped. 'That's impossible. It has been dormant for hundreds of years.'

The young man's expression darkened. 'Not anymore. We were given no warning. One day it was dormant, and then the next it began spouting fire and ash. The mages say it is only a matter of time before it erupts fully and destroys the town.'

Gabriel waved a hand in the direction of the coast. 'Surely the Fire mages and their apprentices would be able to subdue it. Coax it back to sleep.'

'When it first became active, the Fire mages stationed in Haven sought to tame it, and one of their apprentices died in the attempt. Then they sent for reinforcements from the guild. Four Fire mages arrived this morning, with a contingent of enforcers, and they went straight to the volcano to assess the danger. An hour later they returned, and we were ordered to evacuate immediately. They said it was only a precaution, but from the looks on their faces this new attempt was going to fail also. They seek to buy us time.'

Shadows filled his gaze. 'Haven is lost, and we are headed inland, to get as far away from the volcano as possible before it blows. Now, if you will excuse me, I have an urgent matter to attend to before I can re-join my family.' He waved a hand at his front.

Merry scrambled farther away, as Gabriel delayed the young man long enough for her and the others to get clear. Then he re-joined them moments later. They waited until the young man was well and truly out of earshot before discussing the new turn of events.

'It appears I was wrong, in thinking Fire mages would be able to tame a volcano.' Gabriel's tone was bleak. 'If what he said is true, getting your Fire charm will be even more dangerous than before, if not impossible.'

Merry hated the thought of going anywhere near an active volcano, but it had to be done if she was to have any hope of getting her charm. 'I have to get to the focal point before it erupts. But maybe you guys should wait here.'

Gabriel's eyes narrowed. 'You are not going on your own. We're in this together.'

Ellen gave a nod. 'You heard what the man said. There are guild mages and enforcers there. If one of them spots you, they'll try to arrest you. It's too dangerous for you to go on your own. We will all go.'

While Merry didn't really want to go on her own, she also didn't want to put her friends in any more danger. 'The enforcers will be hunting for both of you as well, and it would be easier for one person to sneak past them than three.'

'Four people,' said Kassandra in an icy tone. 'Or did you forget I was here? Not that it matters. You need the charm, and we need to get moving before the damn thing erupts. So stop wasting time.'

Merry shot the enforcer a hard look but didn't argue the point. From the stubborn looks on their faces, none of her friends would agree to stay behind and Kassandra was right that they were running out of time. With speed of the essence, they headed back to the road. The line of evacuees had disappeared round a bend, leaving the road to Haven empty. Without worrying about being spotted, they could travel faster and reached the harbour town's wall within two hours.

There was no sign of the enforcers or mages the young man had mentioned, as they carefully neared the open gates leading into town. When Merry used her Earth sense she could find no sparks to indicate magical or non-magical people inside any of the buildings lining the main road. Much as in Greystone, the road led down to the harbour. The wind brought with it a mixed bag of scents, the crisp smell of the sea, along with a hint of smoke. There were no boats bobbing in the water; no doubt all of them had been used to evacuate the residents.

It was quiet, too quiet. Not even gulls wheeled in the air above the harbour. Just as it had been when she and Ellen had arrived in Marshland.

Merry's skin prickled, a strange current washing over her. It came in waves that set her teeth on edge and made her head buzz. This wasn't like the poisoned aquamarine that had set her stomach churning. It didn't make her feel sick or repel her in any way. It was more as if some immense presence was trying to communicate with her but was using the wrong frequency. She turned around slowly, trying to see if she could improve the reception. When she faced left, the buzz in her ears subsided and warmth built in her solar plexus.

She was not surprised when Gabriel pointed at a cobbled road to the left of the town wall and said, 'The volcano is that way.'

The heat in Merry's middle strengthened as they walked down the road. The current zinging through her body was now constant, making it hard for Merry to focus on her Earth senses to search ahead. It flared and pulsed within her, much like the flames had danced in their campfires each night. With deep breaths, she worked to block out the call of what had to be the Fire

focal point, focusing on the earth beneath the cobble-
stones and imperfections within the stones themselves.

It helped, and she was able to block out the lure of
the focal point, the heat lessening in her body. Up ahead,
her senses caught flashes of red, and she waved for her
friends to conceal themselves in the shadows of the
forest on the other side of the road. They walked
parallel to the road as it curved away from the town
wall. Merry chanted her invisibility spell under her
breath as she led her friends to the last row of trees and
peered through the foliage. On the other side was a large
clearing lined with trees, and a stone sundial in the
centre.

The enforcers Merry had sensed were grouped
around two horse drawn carriages. Some were tending
to the horses who were tethered nearby, while others
rummaged in packs spread out on the ground in front of
the sundial. One stood alone, a hand shielding his eyes
as he peered down a path on the other side of the
cleaning.

'Adrian.' Ellen's whisper carried delight, and her
expression brightened at the sight of him.

Though he had technically helped Merry and Gabriel
escape the tower, she was not as happy as her friend to
see him. He had only let them go because he had a
bigger concern with the traitors to the guild at the time.
Here, there would be nothing to deter him from obeying
his oath if he were to catch sight of them.

But Gabriel was just as happy as Ellen to see his

friend and, after he indicated for Merry and the others to retreat further into the forest, he insisted they try to contact him. 'If nothing else, he will be a source of information,' he said.

'And if he tries to arrest us, what then?' Merry asked.

'Then Ellen can use her magic to put him to sleep.'

Ellen didn't look pleased at the idea of using her magic on Adrian, but she did agree to the plan. Beethoven was sent to capture the enforcer's attention, while Sadie waited at the edge of the forest, allowing Merry to watch what was going on through her eyes. The grey and white cat lithely wended his way through the trees and then sauntered over to tap Adrian on the leg. The enforcer heaved a sigh and shook his head, before gesturing for the cat to lead him onwards.

As Adrian neared the tree-line, Sadie severed the connection between her and Merry. A short time later, both familiars emerged from the trees, with the enforcer a step behind them. At first he gazed around unseeing, until Merry widened her invisibility spell to include him.

Adrian crossed his arms in front of his chest, an expression of exasperation on his face as he eyed Gabriel. 'Why am I not surprised to find you here?' he said as he then inclined his head towards Merry. 'You always turn up wherever there is trouble.'

Before Merry could respond to his assertion that she was a magnet for trouble, Adrian spotted Ellen and a smile overtook his scowl. 'Miss Hayland, it is a pleasure to see you again, though I wish it were in better circumstances.'

Ellen flushed and gave him a smile in return. 'I am pleased to make your acquaintance again, Master Irvine.'

A soft snort came from Kassandra, who was standing behind Merry, and Adrian's expression darkened when he realised she was there. Fists clenched, he moved towards her.

'Traitor.'

Kassandra raised her own hands and the two enforcers stared at one another as the trees around them began to shake.

'Enough.' Merry stepped between them before thinking it through and was buffeted aside by whatever force they were applying against each other. She lost her grip on her invisibility spell, and her connection with the earth fizzled out. Heat flashed through her body as the current from the focal point engulfed her and she dropped to her knees. She dug her fingers into the dirt, reaching out with her Earth magic and imagined a solid rock wall encasing her, blocking out the call of the fire.

'Are you okay?' Ellen gripped Merry's arm and helped her to her feet.

'I'm fine.' Merry gave her friend a quick smile and then looked to where Gabriel stood beside Adrian, a calming hand on his arm.

'It's okay, Adrian. Kassandra is with us,' said Gabriel.

'No, I'm not,' said Kassandra, pushing in front of Merry to glare at Gabriel. 'I'm your prisoner.'

Though thrown by what the focal point was doing to her, Merry rolled her eyes at Kassandra. 'You haven't been tied up or restrained in any way since before we reached Dryton. I think it's time to admit you're with us of your own free will.'

Kassandra whirled around to face her. 'Do you really think this is where I would choose to be, if I had free will? I don't want anything to do with you or your stupid quest. I'm just trying not to get killed.'

Merry stiffened. 'We're not the ones who are threatening your life. That honour belongs to your stupid brother and that megalomaniac lord he's hooked up with. They're the ones putting all of our lives at risk. I've let you hold on to your delusion that you are our prisoner for long enough. It's time to face facts. You know what your brother and Lord Andel are up to is wrong, and you're scared of having your oath bound against your will, putting you in Karl's command forever.'

Some of the anger left Merry at the stricken look on Kassandra's face as her words hit home. 'Look, I know you're scared. Anyone with half a brain would be terrified at the prospect of being completely under someone else's control. Your loyalty to your brother placed you in an impossible situation, and you did the best you could. But you made a choice when you elected to come with us. Like it or not, you're one of us now.'

Kassandra stared at her for a long moment, and then let out a long sigh. 'Fine. Just don't expect me to pretend that I like you. Any of you,' she said as she glared at the rest of them.

Adrian watched all this with a perplexed expression, and then turned to Gabriel. 'Seems you've had an interesting time of it since you escaped the tower. Speaking of which, I am under strict orders to arrest you on sight. Consider yourself arrested and my prisoner.' He gave a wry smirk. 'Much the way Kassandra is your prisoner.'

Gabriel clasped his friend on the shoulder. 'Duly noted. Now, tell us what has been happening here? We heard you evacuated the town and expect the volcano to blow at any moment.'

Adrian's expression darkened. 'It's not the volcano you need to worry about. The Fire focal point is unstable. That's what caused the volcano to awaken. The mages I bought with me are working to subdue it, but ordered Haven be evacuated in case they fail.'

He looked over to Merry. 'There are six mages inside the grotto containing the focal point, as well as a squad of enforcers, so you will have little chance of sneaking in to get your charm without being seen. Mage Fairweather knows what you are after, and even if the mages succeed, and make the volcano dormant again, they have orders to remain in place to ensure you do not get your charm. The Spirit focal point is similarly guarded, and they know you have been using some kind of invisibility spell to remain hidden and have mages more attuned keeping a look out for you.'

Merry's eyes widened as he spelled out the obstacles she faced.

Gabriel reached out to her. 'Don't worry. We will find a way to get you into the grotto once the volcano has been subdued. They may have mages looking for you, but they don't really know all that you are capable of.'

Merry appreciated Gabriel's support, but it wasn't going to be as easy as that, and it would be suicide to enter the volcano if it was on the verge of erupting.

She hadn't needed Adrian to tell her the focal point was unstable. The mental wall she had built around her consciousness was blocking it out for now, but she could still sense the element fighting for a way in. It called to her, its cries becoming increasingly frenzied. All it would take was one spark breaking through and she would be lost in the flames. She was no mage, trained to withstand the full force of elemental magic. To get her charm she needed to be there, at the focal point, where the pressure to give in to the flames would be unbearable.

Still, she had to try.

With a tight grip on her mental wall, Merry cast out her senses, looking for a gap in the guild's cordon around the volcano. There had to be a way she and her friends could slip through. As she drew closer to the volcano itself, she found enforcers stationed at the entrance to the grotto. She could sense the Fire mages within the grotto, 'see' the trail of their magic as they worked to calm the focal point. But there was no sign of the mages Adrian had said were on the lookout for her. If they were able to use an invisibility spell like hers, they could be anywhere.

Merry turned to Kassandra. 'Are you sure your brother isn't behind this?' She waved a hand towards the volcano. 'I can't detect a poison stone, like in Marshland, but it could be something different.'

Kassandra frowned. 'I already told you, Karl did not share his plans with me. All I know is that he and Lord Andel wanted to spread as much havoc and chaos as they could, to keep the guild busy and to make it easier for them to seize control.'

Merry grimaced. The havoc they'd so far created had killed many people. Andel and Karl had no regard for the loss of life caused by their schemes, and she did not think that would change if they gained control of Tirana. In their own way, they could be worse than the guild and make the place even weaker when the witch hunters arrived. She had to stop that from happening. But to do that she needed the Fire charm.

She turned back to survey the volcano, this time focusing on what the Fire mages were doing. Maybe she could find a way to help them subdue the focal point. That would give her one fewer thing to worry about once she found a way to get her charm.

From what she could sense of their magic, it appeared they were seeking to draw power away from the focal point. Gregor had taught her how to reduce the heat put out by a campfire, but the skill involved in this undertaking was breathtaking. The flows of their magic glowed as they interweaved to form a delicate lace around the dancing flame in the centre of the grotto. The longer she studied what the Fire mages were doing the more she realised how out of her league she was.

Dampening the flames of a campfire was one thing, draining the energy from an elemental focal point another thing entirely. But if that was what she had to do, then she would find a way.

CHAPTER 12

A focal point that became unstable with no warning seemed suspicious. Magic had to be behind it. If Merry could neutralise the magic then they had a better chance of succeeding.

But no matter which of her magical senses she used, she could detect nothing that appeared out of place within the grotto itself. What she could sense was a weakening of the magical threads being woven by the Fire mages. They were tiring, and as soon as their efforts failed the instability in the focal point would increase.

If Merry didn't get her charm soon, she might never be able to. Somehow, she had to get past the enforcers and invisible mages guarding the way to the volcano. She pulled out her heartstone, but this time she focused on the volcano itself, looking for a way in that wasn't guarded.

Her Earth sense quickly found the route the Fire mages had used, the path well-travelled. There were other smaller tunnels, ancient lava tubes, in the heart of the volcano, but any big enough for a person to enter had an enforcer stationed nearby. Merry would be able to use her magic to enlarge one of the tubes, but that would surely alert the mages hunting her.

Despite the odds against her piling up, she refused to give up, her consciousness following the path of every lava tube until she found one that would get her close to the grotto before she would have to use magic to carve the rest of the way. The lava tube opened onto a tiny sandbar at the base of a cliff that jutted out over the ocean.

'I can't get to the focal point from here,' said Merry, pulling her senses back from exploring the volcano. 'It's too well guarded. There's only one way that might work.' She filled them in on what she had found.

'How are you supposed to reach it? They've taken all the boats,' said Ellen.

Merry scanned the harbour with her senses, hoping the evacuees had missed one. Or maybe there would be a boat in dry dock, awaiting repairs, that they could use. It would have to be one that was not in as bad a condition as the one she and Ellen had used in Marshland Province when they were fleeing the dam. With Gabriel's help, they might be able to repair one and get closer to the shore side of the volcano, without either of them having to magically exhaust themselves.

But from what she could tell, there were no boats left behind. Anything that could float had been put to use by the people fleeing the imminent eruption. They would have to find another way to get through the cordon of enforcers and guild mages blocking access to the volcano.

Merry had started to give her friends the bad news, when a flash of light to the left caught her attention. The life sparks of dozens of people with magic flared in her mind's eye when she concentrated her senses on them. At first she thought they might be more guild mages, but these people were heading away from the volcano. Most of them were the pale life sparks of witches with a variety of affinities, but one shone with a bright purple light. Merry focused her senses on what had to be a Spirit mage.

A grin curved her lips when she recognised the vibrant spark.

'I've found Donna Syphera,' she said as she opened her eyes. 'She and a group of witches are heading in that direction.' Merry pointed into the dense forest.

'Mage Syphera is here?' Adrian frowned. He was no doubt remembering his last encounter with the renegade mage.

'Don't even think about trying to arrest her,' said Merry, hands on her hips. 'We need her help.'

'How is a Spirit mage going to help us?' asked Gabriel. 'From what you said, we would need Earth, Fire and Water mages to get to the other side of the volcano.'

'We do, but Donna has something else we need. At least, I hope she does.' Merry once again sent out her senses, this time in the direction Donna and the others were headed.

There, a short distance away from the sparks that represented Donna and the witches, she found what she was looking for.

'The *Hellcat* is anchored in a cove not far from here,' said Merry. 'If we can get there before they sail away, we can ask Captain Higgins to sail us to the coast side of the volcano. Gabriel and I can speed the trip with wind, and I'm sure the witches Donna has with her can help us scale the cliff and get to the fire focal point without being caught.'

'I'm coming too,' said Adrian, a scowl darkening his expression. 'Gabriel is my prisoner, as are you. Where you go, I go.'

Gabriel and Ellen were pleased with his statement, but Merry shared a sceptical glance with Kassandra. Though she hated to think she had anything in common with the rogue enforcer, Merry was glad to see she wasn't the only one suspicious of Adrian's motives. This loophole of his, to prevent him from obeying his oath to the guild, seemed too convenient. If it was that easy to get out of obeying, no one would be worried about being oath bound. For Ellen's sake, she hoped her suspicions proved false. In the meantime, she would watch her back around the enforcer. For now though, she had to focus on getting to the cove before Captain Higgins pulled up anchor and sailed away.

Sadie, how far does your range extend? Can you talk to Donna and ask her to wait for us?

The black cat had been able to communicate with Merry from a distance while they were fleeing the tower.

I can communicate with you over longer distances, because of our bond. I would need to be closer to be able to reach Donna. At this stage, I am unable to even sense her presence, but I will send your request through as soon as I am able. We'd better hurry though; there is little time to waste. I may not be able to reach Donna, but I can feel the instability in the land. Whatever those mages are doing to subdue the fire focal point is weakening, and I fear soon we will have more to deal with than just an erupting volcano.

Merry agreed, her senses going haywire thanks to all the magic being expended. She could also sense the instability in the Fire focal point even with her mental wall in place. It twanged on her senses, making her feel extra sensitive, as if her skin was being scoured by a harsh brush from the inside out. It was not a pleasant feeling at all.

It was hard to go fast with dense bush between them and the cove, though Merry ranged ahead with her Earth senses to find the quickest and least cluttered route. But with the Fire focal point practically screaming in her ear it was hard to concentrate for long periods of time. In the end she had to stop and let Sadie pick their path. The familiar was attuned to the Earth due to her nature and this helped spare Merry's magical nerves somewhat.

A quick glance revealed her companions did not seem affected, most likely due to not having an affinity to Fire. Lucky them.

As she wended her way through tree trunks and around bushes, Merry tried to connect with her Fire side, to see if she could soothe it somehow. But it was too volatile and doing so made her head ache. As she figured she would need all her energy to stop the volcano erupting, Merry gave up and just concentrated on going as fast as she could, reinforcing her mental wall to block out the distressed call of the focal point.

As they drew near the shoreline, the trees became sparse, making it easier going, at least until the soil changed to sand and began to suck at Merry's feet. Her companions seemed equally challenged, though both familiars skimmed lightly across the surface.

They were almost at the entrance to the cove, when Sadie announced she had been able to communicate with Donna.

I didn't give her all the details, just told her that we were on our way and needed to speak with her urgently.

'I'm not surprised to see you here,' said Donna, when Merry and her friends clambered over a sand dune and met the Spirit mage on the beach, 'but I was not expecting your companions.' She indicated behind Merry. 'A guild mage and two enforcers. One of which tried to arrest both of us last time we met.' She eyed Adrian. 'I hope you are not going to attempt something so foolish once again. With only one enforcer on your side, you are in an even worse position than you were before, and I'm not inclined to be as lenient as I was then.'

Adrian grimaced at Donna's thinly veiled threat, but he shook his head. 'I have no interest in arresting you. I have far more important concerns at present.'

Donna's eyebrows rose, and she looked about to argue with him some more, but Merry cut her off.

'The Fire mages are losing control of the focal point. If we don't do something soon, the volcano is going to erupt. I need your help, and *Hellcat*, to get to the focal point and get my charm before that happens.'

Donna turned to Merry. 'Do you think that is wise? The swiftness of the volcano going from dormant to active is suspicious, and the witches among us with Fire magic have said the element is unsettled. You would be better off fleeing with us.'

Unsettled was an understatement. But Merry didn't have time to go into that. 'I need that charm, and I think there might be a way to settle the focal point. But it will take all the elements.' In as few words as possible she explained her plan. 'I need you to convince Captain Higgins to help us. The only way I can get close enough to the focal point to make a difference is onboard the *Hellcat*.'

Donna frowned. 'Captain Higgins has a well-developed sense of self preservation. She will not be happy to risk her ship. As you said, the volcano could blow at any moment and being at sea will not save us.'

Merry pointed to the witches assembled behind Donna. 'We can do this. Together. If we don't, the risk to the rest of Tirana could be catastrophic. The Fire focal point is approaching flashpoint. Once it explodes no one will be able to contain it, and that will have an effect on all the other elements. Tirana sits on a tectonic shelf made up of four plates. The elemental focal points line up with the fault lines. If this volcano erupts, it will cause a chain reaction that could destroy Tirana.'

Merry didn't know if Donna understood the terminology she was using. While Tirana might be magically advanced, she had seen little evidence of Earth based science.

Sadie, can you share these images with Donna?

Merry pictured news reports from back home of the destruction caused by erupting volcanoes, earthquakes and tsunamis, and what she could remember of high school geology lessons.

As she watched, the Spirit mage's face paled.

Finally, Donna's expression firmed. 'I will make Captain Higgins see reason.'

With a sigh of relief, Merry indicated for her friends to follow the mage to the shoreline. The familiar rowing boats waited to ferry them all to the *Hellcat*, though Merry noticed none of the witches wanted to get close to Adrian or Kassandra. Both enforcers wore matching sour expressions as they ended up side by side at the bow of one of the boats, with the witches huddled down the other end. Ellen and Gabriel, Sadie and Beethoven joined the enforcers, and Merry did as well, to even up the weight distribution. It was not because that was where she wanted to be. She still didn't trust Adrian's way of working around his oath. He showed no signs of the distress he'd displayed back at the guild tower, when he'd been resisting the urge to stop her and Gabriel from escaping, but there was no time to spare to figure out what was really going on. Stopping the focal point from exploding and setting off the volcano had to be her first priority.

Merry was thankful not to be dripping wet and coated in sand this time around as she scaled the rope ladder slung over the side of the *Hellcat* and then clambered over the railing. With Donna at her side, she strode to where Captain Higgins stood at the helm beside her first mate.

Captain Higgins tilted her head back and narrowed her eyes. 'Why do I get the feeling this is not going to be as swift and easy an escape as I would like?'

'Because you may not have magic, but you know the sea. You know had bad this is.' Merry pointed in the direction of the volcano. 'I need you to take me there before all hope is lost.' Once again, she gave a brief explanation of the problem.

'With two Air mages on board, I should be getting you to speed our way clear of here. Yet you want to use your magic to sail us directly into danger. You want me to risk *Hellcat* on the chance that you might be able to stop a focal point from exploding and a volcano from erupting. Last time I saw you, you had Earth, Water and Air magic. Now suddenly you're a Fire mage?'

Merry shook her head. 'I don't know what I am. But I do know that nowhere in Tirana will be safe, on land or at sea, if we don't stop the Fire focal point reaching flashpoint.'

'Merry is right,' said Donna. 'Saving Tirana is more important than saving your own skin. You might be able to outrun the volcano for now, but you have nowhere safe to run to. Might as well make your stand here.'

For a long moment, Captain Higgins didn't respond. Then, after a long and drawn-out sigh, she turned to her first mate and said, 'You heard the mage, get *Hellcat* moving.'

In short order the *Hellcat* was sailing away from the cove, though in the end it was three of the Air witches who helped fill the sails with wind.

Gabriel and Merry were resting ahead of the coming fight.

It would be a fight. There was no way the guild forces were going to let them just sail in and waltz up to the focal point, even if they were coming to help.

As the *Hellcat* cleared the edge of the cove and sailed into deep water, heading in the direction of the volcano, opposing wind began to buffet the ship from all directions, even as the sea around them began to churn.

Witches cried out as the ship lurched from side to side, grabbing hold of rigging and rails to stop themselves from being tumbled around. Yet, even as they did this the witches began to fight back. While the Air witches concentrated on pushing the ship forward, Water witches worked to settle the sea and Earth witches tended to injuries and ailments caused by the rough passage.

Merry wanted to join in and help them but knew her focus was needed elsewhere. She left it to Gabriel to assist the Air and Water witches and instead sent her senses ranging ahead, trying to find out where the attack was coming from. There was no way it was natural.

She couldn't see or sense anything. The ocean was clear all around the *Hellcat*. No clouds marred the crystal blue sky and the water a short distance beyond the ship was relatively calm. It didn't make sense. What was she missing?

Gripping the railing in both hands, feet spread, and knees bent to aid her balance, Merry narrowed her eyes and scanned the calm seas beyond the maelstrom that surrounded the ship. 'Show me,' she said, willing whatever was hidden to become clear.

Nothing happened, so she repeated the words again and again. Pressure built in her head, as it did when she had to focus to strengthen her invisibility spell, and the air shimmered in the distance. She risked freeing one hand to grip her heartstone and pitted her strength against the magic users working to conceal themselves from her magical sight. The shimmer became a rainbow of colours, representing all the elements. It wasn't one mage she was fighting against, but many magic users linked together. Sweat coated Merry's face, even as her legs threatened to buckle, Even with her heartstone, she was not strong enough.

Then a hand gripped her right shoulder, while another gripped her left. As more hands were placed on Merry's arms and back, energy flooded her body.

Spirit. Earth. Air. Fire. Water. Power from each element flowed into her. This was not a link like the one she and Gabriel had used against the poisoned stone at the Water focal point. This was witches offering up their strength, bolstering Merry's energy with their own.

She straightened up, energy coursing through every inch of her body as she shouted. 'SHOW ME!'

The shimmer burst and a ship came into sharp focus, the railing lined with magic users. Merry could see their faces clearly, though they were hundreds of metres away, the power thrumming through her enhancing her vision. More, she could see the bluish-purple hue of heartstones glimmering in the air around their heads.

Oath bound witches, caught up in Lord Andel's scheme to become King.

With the power she had been gifted, Merry could smash their ship to smithereens, but this was not their fault. Most of them would have been forced to make the oath.

She called out to Gabriel where he stood at the bow of the ship. 'We need to blow them off course, get them out of our way.'

He ran to her side, with the witches that had gifted her energy moving so he could take her hand. Then, together, they whipped up a wind and sent it at the ship. Merry winced as the ship was tossed about, pained cries coming from the witches at the railings, but she didn't let her wind ease until she and Gabriel had forced the ship a good distance away.

The wind was so ferocious, the sails of the other ship were in tatters by the time they were done. Then Merry shouted for Captain Higgins to steer them towards the cliff once more. With some of the Air witches speeding their way, while Water witches made sure the enemy ship could not regain its equilibrium, they raced to the cliff face that sheltered the volcano. Now that Andel's people were not obscuring Merry's physical and magical sight, she could see what it was they had been doing.

The instability in the Fire focal point was as unnatural as the storm that had almost sunk the *Hellcat*.

Not a poison stone.

Magic had carved channels into the side of the volcano, forming a lattice in the rock that glowed with the colours of all five elements. The living spell would have been breathtaking if the outcome wasn't so deadly. The Fire component of the spell was feeding the volcano, heating the magma at its core, while Air fanned the flames. Earth was creating new pathways for the spell as it stretched towards the grotto where the guild mages fought a losing battle to contain the focal point, and Water sucked out any hint of moisture. Spirit was the glue holding the spell together.

The closer *Hellcat* got to the volcano, the more the spell pinged on Merry's senses, and she could feel it pulling at her, seeking to use her magic to bolster its power now she had removed the magic users who had created it. Each attempt she made to stop the spell was thwarted. She needed mages from all the elements, working together, to sever each element at the same time. She was strongest in Earth and had Donna for Spirit, and Gabriel for Air and Water, but her fledging ability with Fire would not be enough.

She explained what she needed from Donna and Gabriel, and then turned to Adrian. 'Is there any way you can contact the Fire mages at the volcano? I need one of them to work with us, to have any hope of stopping this spell.' She refused to contemplate not being able to stop it. Everything depended on her succeeding.

Adrian shook his head. 'I've no talent for Spirit, and none of the mages has a winged familiar.'

Merry turned to Donna, before he'd even finished talking.

Expression determined, the Spirit mage asked, 'What mages are in the grotto?'

Adrian listed several names, and Donna gave a nod. 'Mage Barrowman has a minor talent for Spirit. I'll give her your message.'

Donna's eyes closed, and her brow furrowed as she reached out to contact the other mage. A whisper swelled around Merry, and she could almost hear Donna's mental voice, though it was too soft and indistinct for her to pick out words. It was more like hearing the Spirit mage's emotions, the whisper carrying a sense of urgency. There was a long moment before a second whisper curled through the air, this one tasting of disbelief and scorn.

Merry didn't need Donna to tell her that Mage Barrowman had not been receptive.

'She doesn't believe I am trying to help. She thinks I'm with that lot.' Donna indicated over her shoulder, to the broken ship still being kept at bay by the Air and Water witches aboard the *Hellcat*.

Merry turned to Adrian. 'How do we convince the guild mages that we are not their enemy?'

Adrian stilled a moment, and then he straightened his shoulders as he faced Donna. 'Tell Mage Barrowman that I have the full authority of the guild to enact this protocol, and to confirm this password with Branstone.' He rattled off a short phrase.

After a tense wait, Mage Barrowman's begrudging acceptance came.

Merry wasted no time. She placed a hand on Donna's arm, visualising the heart of the spell, where the five elements intertwined to create an anchor point. She wrapped her senses around the Earth thread, not daring to breathe as Gabriel and the others did the same to their elements. This had to work.

'Now.' She exhaled on the word as Earth magic poured out of her, delving deep into the anchor point. She could sense the magic of the others as they did the same, smothering the threads in their own magic. Then, they began to pull, wresting their element away from the others.

'It's working,' she heard someone shout out nearby. 'The spell is fading.'

Sweat dripped down the sides of Merry's face, and her entire body trembled, legs threatening to collapse under her. She clung to the ship's railing to keep herself upright. A firm touch on her shoulder came seconds before fresh energy flowed into her, from Ellen and the other Earth witches. She was able to straighten up, ready for one last ditch effort to neutralise the spell, her hope buoyed up by sensing that the Fire focal point had begun to stabilise.

The lattice spell gave one last pulse and then it gave way, crumpling to dust.

Exultation filled Merry. They'd done it. Without the rebels' spell interfering, the Fire mages would be able to stabilise the focal point and stop the volcano from erupting.

Even as she had the thought, Merry's sense of the Fire mage's magic winked out, agony ripping through her head.

What the hell?

Merry opened her eyes, seeing matching pained expressions on Gabriel and Donna's faces as they rubbed their temples.

The Spirit mage's face was pale. 'I can't reach Mage Barrowman. It's as if her spirit is no longer there.'

Though it hurt her head to even think about using magic again, Merry reached out with her Earth sense, seeking the life sparks of the Fire mages in the grotto.

Had her plan succeeded, only to lead to Mage Barrowman's death?

CHAPTER 13

*S*ix orange sparks shone in Merry's mind, clustered around the focal point, but her relief at finding all the Fire mages alive was short lived. The mages were surrounded by the sparks of magic users of all elements and strengths. One spark stood out among them, the blue and purple of the black-haired man who worked for Lord Andel. The man with the perverted heartstones.

Horror filled Merry as one of the Fire mage's bright orange sparks dulled, smothered in blue and purple swirls. A stream of Fire magic shot out of the subverted mage, hitting the focal point and setting it into a frenzied dance, even as the spark of one of the other mages began to dim. In her head, Merry could hear the fresh screams of the flame that represented the focal point. It writhed as it was lashed again and again, pushing it towards flashpoint once more.

Merry wrenched her consciousness back and turned to face her friends. How was she going to tell them that their efforts had been in vain? Even now the black-haired man was using his heartstones to bind the Fire mages' oaths to force them to whip the Fire focal point into a frenzy, and any headway they had gained was rapidly being eaten away. Soon it would be too late, with everyone in the vicinity incinerated when it reached flashpoint.

As she filled her friends in on what was taking place inside the grotto, Adrian glowered at her, crossing his arms in front of his chest.

'That's impossible,' he said. 'My enforcers would never let Andel's renegades near the mages.'

Merry spread her hands. 'I'm just telling you what I saw.' In the multitude of sparks she'd seen surrounding the Fire mages, none of them blazed with the red that indicated they were telekinetic. She also couldn't tell if any of them were the mages Adrian had said had been on the lookout for her.

'They could be hidden by an invisibility spell, by the other mages you brought with you,' said Ellen as she placed a soothing hand on Adrian's arm.

'That still wouldn't explain how the rogue Singer and his people were able to infiltrate the grotto,' said Gabriel. 'We have to assume your enforcers have been neutralised in some way.' He gave his friend an apologetic shrug.

Some of the heat left Adrian's gaze, only to be

replaced with determination. Merry knew he realised the same thing she did. Retreat was not an option. Neither was failure. They had to get to the focal point before it imploded, and if that meant having to go up against his colleagues, then that was what they had to do. Every second it took them to get to the focal point gave the black-haired man longer to subdue the guild Fire mages and bind their oaths with his perverted heartstones.

The witches onboard the *Hellcat*, who had helped to get Merry and her friends this far, were exhausted. They would not be able to aid her in the coming fight. The thought that they might be racing to go up against double the trouble without them sat heavily, but it didn't change anything. They had to continue.

Merry scanned the side of the volcano below the lattice spell, focusing on the lava tube just above the water line as Captain Higgins steered the *Hellcat* closer. Using Earth and Water, she scooped up wide swathes of sand from beneath the ship, pushing it onto the tiny sandbar to enlarge it and raise it to the same height as the lava tube.

'Hurry up and launch the longboats,' she called out to the first mate.

Conscious of time running out, Merry climbed over the ship's railing and started to descend the rope ladder as the first longboat was lowered to the water. She clambered aboard as soon as it landed, and then chafed at the delay as Gabriel, Ellen, Kassandra, Adrian, the two familiars and Donna joined her. The sailors didn't need to row with Gabriel using Air to speed the boat to the sandbar.

As soon as they drew close enough, Merry jumped out of the boat, her boots sinking in the damp sand. She set off at a run for the lava tube. This close to the focal point, intense waves of heat washed over her body, drowning out her other senses. But Merry already knew the lava tube would lead them closer to their destination. She commanded her staff to light up and was about to dive into the opening when Sadie called out a warning.

Merry skidded to a halt and eyed the jumble of sand-coloured rocks that littered the floor of the lava tube. They were fist sized, fairly uniform in shape but otherwise unremarkable. One of the rocks, the one closest to Merry, quivered. Not a rock then. As she watched, eight long appendages unwound from beneath it as the quivering increased. The spider shuffled around and fixed its beady eyes on Merry as the rocks just behind it started to quiver.

There were more spiders, all of them unwinding their long legs and turning to face Merry and her friends. With a firm grip on her staff, she worked to block out her sense of the focal point and focus on the spiders. They all shone with an orange glow and Merry could pick out dozens more of them within the depths of the lava tube. All of them started to move towards the opening onto the sandbar where she and her friends stood.

They are infernae spiders. Their bite will inflict excruciating pain on their victims as their bodies burn from the inside out. There is no cure.

Merry's stomach lurched. *How are we supposed to fight them?* There was no time to find another way through.

Their armoured bodies are impervious to fire, and the Fire mage who created them ensured they are resistant to the other elements as well. Killing them will not be an easy task, but you had better do something quickly. They were designed to seek out and eliminate magic users with elements other than Fire.

Even as Sadie said this, the first group of spiders burst out of the tube's opening and scurried across the sandbar towards Merry and her friends. She quickly flung out a wind wall to knock them back, even as she could hear Gabriel telling the others about the danger and calling for them to get behind Merry.

Anyone with Fire magic is safe, but Sadie is right. You need to do something fast. You will not be able to hold them off indefinitely.

Merry grimaced at Beethoven's words, even as she strengthened her wind wall. The first row of spiders had flattened themselves to the sand as they crept forward, while more of them poured from the lava tube, spreading out as they sought a gap in her defences. They would be surrounded by the cursed things in no time, and there was no way she would be able to stop them from attacking her friends indefinitely. At the thought of one of the spiders sinking its fangs into Ellen or Gabriel, Merry gritted her teeth. She would not let that happen.

Anger burned in her belly, and she fanned the flames, seeking to reach the part of herself that represented her Fire magic. She had been able to harness it under Gregor's tutoring, and she would do so here, to save her friends.

The heat in her solar plexus grew, almost matching the intensity she could feel pouring out of the focal point.

She fed on it, let it build up inside her as the *infernae* crept closer. A Fire mage had created them. A potential Fire mage was going to stop them.

She let go of her wind as she stepped forward, waving her staff at the spiders as she mentally commanded them to stop. Heat poured out of her, hitting the first row of spiders. They shuddered a moment before lurching forwards once more.

Merry gritted her teeth and roared at them in her head. *I SAID STOP!*

Her staff lit up brighter than it ever had before and the front row of spiders froze mid-step, some of them toppling sideways. The ones behind scrambled over top of the frozen ones, but as light flared out from Merry's staff in a widening wave these also came to a lurching stop. Soon all of the spiders that were pouring out of the opening were frozen in place.

Eyes wide, Merry turned to her friends. 'We need to go. Now. I have no idea how long this will hold them.'

They hurried through the spiders, careful not to step on any of them. Merry shuddered to think what would happen if any of them became unfrozen while she and the others were in their midst. She had to step carefully to avoid treading on any of them. They littered the floor of the lava tube, making it hard going, but with her staff still blazing she didn't have to worry about being left in the dark.

The deeper she went into the tunnel the brighter it got, until it hurt to look at it. She squinted to protect her eyes from the glare. With whatever it was doing to keep the spiders immobile, there was no way she was going to stop it from blazing. There were holes in the sides of the tube, and spiders poked out of some of them and in others she could hear the skitter of hundreds of tiny feet drawing closer. More spiders, ones that weren't frozen. Were they out of the staff's range?

'We need to hurry up,' she said in a quiet voice, increasing her pace. Her feet brushed against a spider as she stepped past a whole bunch of them tangled together and the leg of one of them twitched. At the same time, her staff pulsed in her hand, the wood warming.

The heat that had been building in her solar plexus pulsed in time with the staff.

It had to be a warning; one she was not about to ignore.

As the skittering in the smaller lava tubes grew louder, Merry started to run, calling out for her friends to do the same. The spiders carpeting the floor of the tunnel were all twitching now. The staff was still blazing, but Merry could sense magic in the air around her. Fire magic.

One of the mages inside the grotto, one whose spark was smothered in blue and purple, was trying to wake the spiders. The ones on the ground around Merry's feet were now shaking as their bodies fought two different compulsions.

They had to get out of the tunnel before the subverted Fire mage wrested full control from Merry.

She could see a large opening ahead and sprinted to the end to scan the next cavern. There was no sign of holes in the walls and the space was free of spiders. She flattened herself against the side of the tunnel as she urged her friends to hurry up. Adrian and Kassandra were in the lead, with the others a little way behind them. They were going to make it. Merry just had to hold the spiders back for a few more seconds.

Ellen cried out as some of the spiders at her feet regained the use of their legs and surged towards her.

Near the end of the tunnel, Adrian spun around, fists clenched as he used his ability to sweep the spiders away from Ellen and force them against the wall. Kassandra stopped as well, hands raised with palms facing the sides of the tunnel, holding back the ones threatening to leap out of the holes in the wall as Ellen hurried past.

Then, side by side, the two enforcers walked backwards along the tunnel to the opening. Gabriel grabbed both of them by an arm and wrenched them backwards as Merry pulled down the ceiling of the tunnel closest to the opening, sealing the spiders inside.

Heart racing, breath coming in gasps, Merry wanted to sink to the floor and rest. But there was no time. She might have blocked off this tunnel, but the spiders could have other ways out. They would not be safe until they were out of the spiders' territory.

The pulsing in her staff and body indicated the Fire focal point was nearby, and she allowed it to lead her onwards, calling for her friends to follow.

'Do you have a plan, for when you reach the focal point?' Kassandra asked as she cast a sideways glance at Merry as they crossed the large cavern. 'Your usual habit of blundering in and hoping for the best isn't going to be enough against six trained Fire mages.'

Merry grimaced at Kassandra's bluntness. Not that the enforcer was wrong. As Merry had told Gregor, everything she had done with her magic so far had been instinctive. How was she supposed to compete with guild mages who had potentially been oath bound by Lord Andel's rebels? She had no training and was seriously outnumbered. Even worse, she might have to fight while trying to stop the black-haired man from compelling her with his song.

'I don't have time to figure out a plan.' She filled the enforcer and her friends in on what was happening.

Kassandra gave a snort as she shook her head. 'It's a miracle you're still alive.'

Merry didn't disagree with her. She just hoped another miracle eventuated between now and when they arrived at the grotto. She was exhausted from everything she had done to get them this far, and her companions were in no better shape. Still, none of them complained as she pushed onwards.

The heat in her solar plexus intensified the closer she got to the Fire focal point, coming in increasing waves as the instability grew. It was so close to blowing that it was drowning out all her other senses. The focal point was screaming as the Fire mages who had previously been trying to stabilise it now fed it.

Merry was running before she realised it, the element's cry for help coursing through her body.

How could the Fire mages stand it, even if they were oath bound to obey Andel's demands? Her nerve endings twitched, sending fiery shocks through her body that set her teeth on edge and brought tears to her eyes. She waved her staff at the wall blocking her access to the focal point and unlaced a wave of Earth, carving out an opening. Without breaking stride, Merry burst through the gap she had made and into the grotto, so desperate to stop the pain that she forgot all about the enemy waiting within. A sharp tug on her arm pulled her back as a projectile flashed in front of her face. Wind whooshed in front of her and dozens more projectiles were dashed to the sides of the grotto.

With Gabriel and the enforcers working to keep her safe, Merry scanned the grotto.

In the very centre, in a stone basin atop a marble pedestal, elemental Fire flickered in an erratic dance. Six Fire mages encircled the pedestal, facing it, the spells they cast drowned out by the crackle of flames. But Merry didn't need to hear what they were saying to know what was happening.

The spells were warping the focal point, whipping it into a flaming frenzy, feeding it with every ounce of their energy. The orange spark that was their magic faded with each passing second, while the blue purple spark that was the perverted heartstones that bound them in thrall grew brighter. There was no sign of the black-haired man or the rest of Andel's forces. Their part was done, and she was sure they had got as far away from here as they could, to avoid the coming explosion of energy. Not that it would do them any good.

Gabriel spun Merry around to face him, and then cupped her face. 'You have to focus. Fight it.'

Merry shook her head, jaw clenched so tight she couldn't speak the words.

How?

How was she to fight the torrent of energy flooding through her body from the Fire focal point? It demanded action, called for her to leap to its defence. It was at breaking point. If she didn't do something soon, it would explode and destroy everything in the immediate vicinity in an instant and then go on to devour the surrounding land within minutes. Nothing could withstand it, or the devastating earthquakes that would follow.

Tirana would be torn asunder.

She pulled free of Gabriel's grasp and lunged away when he tried to grab her again, fire blossoming in a circle around her to ward him off.

He raised his arms to shield his face from the heat of the flames that surrounded her, sweat sheening his skin. He called her name, anguish in his tone, even as he summoned wind to try to force the flames back. The flames surrounding Merry intensified; the air between her and her friends shimmering with it as Adrian grabbed Gabriel's arm and pulled him away from immediate danger. The enforcer pulled the struggling mage back with him as he retreated to the wall of the grotto, to where the rest of her friends waited.

Ellen's eyes were filled with horror and even Kassandra looked worried, while Sadie and Beethoven implored Merry to see sense. She blocked out their mental voices. This was her fight. She was the only one able to enter the grotto and not be burned to a crisp.

She sucked in a breath and then darted under the linked arms of the Fire mages. They did not respond as she launched herself into the centre of the grotto, the flames welcoming her.

Merry gave herself over to the Fire, feeling it caress every inch of her body, the resonance throbbing through her soul. She closed her eyes and held out her arms, wrapped in an embrace that seared and yet soothed. There was no separation between her and the focal point. She was the Fire.

Dimly she was aware of the Fire mages, their sparks so dim they would be extinguished in seconds, becoming empty husks. With a wave of her arms, she severed the conduits of fire that flowed from within her to the mages. They fell to the ground, robes smoking, while the heartstones that had bound them hovered in the air above them. Merry reached out with fingers of fire and plucked the stones from the air, melding them together to form one stone.

The blue and purple swirls within the stone caught alight, the colour changing to a vibrant mix of orange and red that darkened as the fire consumed the magic at the heart of the stone. As her friends rushed to tend to the fallen mages, she focused on the flame that writhed through the stone. It matched the one building inside her.

She was incandescent.

She was Fire.

Nothing else existed.

Merry, do not lose yourself to the flame. You must fight it. You mut take control.

Merry shook her head, forcing Sadie's voice aside. She had no need to fight. Every thought she had, the Fire obeyed, and with her new firestone she sent it twirling through the air around her, laughing as it danced at her command. This was nothing like when she had become a conduit for the Earth tree, waging destruction on everything around her.

This was bliss.

With the firestone she had nothing to fear, no doubts to overcome. She could do anything. Be anything. No more hiding from the guild or worrying about how she was going to stop Lord Andel from plunging Tirana into civil war, and if *Huntingdon Inc.* found a way through the portal and attempted to persecute witches she could easily stop them. With Fire at her command, Tirana and her friends would be safe, and anyone who stood against her would burn.

You do not need flame to save Tirana. You are Merry Meadows, my companion. Your strength and your compassion is what will see us through. No one need burn. All we need is you, Merry, I have already lost Meredith. I will not lose you as well.

A sharp sting flared in the wrist that held the fire-stone and she shook her hand. The stone tumbled free, falling to the ground at Merry's feet even as the flames that surrounded her were extinguished. She reeled, dizzied by the loss of the flame within.

'Sadie.'

Ellen's anguished cry reverberated in Merry's head. She spun around and saw the little cat lying on the ground, charred sections of fur on her head and body.

'No.' She dropped to her knees beside the familiar, hands stretching out. Then she pulled them back, not wanting to make it worse by touching her. 'I'm so sorry, Sadie. I didn't mean to burn you.'

It wasn't you. Sadie's mental voice was faint and threaded with pain. *You would never hurt me.*

She got burned when she bit you, to break you from your trance.

Tears stung Merry's eyes at Beethoven's words. Then she looked to Ellen. 'Can you help her?'

The healer kneeled on the other side of Sadie, hand already clasping her heartstone, determination replacing the anguish of before. 'I'll do my best.'

Goosebumps washed over Merry's skin as the healer worked her magic. Gabriel stepped to her side and placed a hand on her shoulder, but she brushed it aside. She didn't deserve comfort. Sadie was hurt because of her. When she'd been enthralled by the Fire focal point she had thought it was the answer to everything, that it would help her protect those she cared about. Instead it had hurt Sadie, and there was no telling what more damage she could have caused if the black cat hadn't intervened.

There is always a price involved when seeking a charm from a focal point, one that takes a heavy toll. But all will be well. Ellen is a fine healer. I feel much better already.

Sadie's voice was stronger, and as Merry watched on her wounds closed over, leaving pale skin exposed where the fur had been seared. But Merry was not comforted. If Ellen had not been there, or hadn't had her renewed heartstone to strengthen her healing spells, Sadie could have died from her injuries.

Enough. Sadie stood up and stalked over to Merry, yellow eyes slitted. *No more guilt. You would do whatever it takes to save me if the situation were reversed. Indeed, you have saved my life many times over since I dragged you to Tirana. Do not take blame for my choices. I am your companion, and you are my witch.*

Her tough stance softened, and she rubbed her head against Merry's knee. *We are a team, and a good one at that.*

Merry gave her companion a watery smile as she stretched out a hand to softly stroke Sadie's silky ears. 'Yes, we are the best team.' She looked up and smiled at her friends. Ellen had been with her from the start, while Gabriel had proved his worth over and over again since they'd met. Donna, Adrian, and even Kassandra had shown that when it came to what was best for Tirana, they would fight alongside her.

That fight could not be won with Fire alone.

With a sigh, Merry plucked up her newest charm and got to her feet. 'It's time to go and get my Spirit charm.'

Easy to say, harder to do. But somehow she would make it work.

CHAPTER 14

*G*etting to the guild tower to claim Merry's spirit charm was easier said than done. They couldn't go back the way they had come as the tunnel they'd used was blocked off, not to mention filled with hundreds of *infernae*. She might have a firestone now, but she was exhausted, as were the others, and in no condition to fight off a spider attack. They would have to take the long way around to get to the cove. Donna was sure Captain Higgins would be happy to sail them to Crystal Harbour, cutting days off their journey.

First though, they had to do something with the guild mages who had been subverted by Lord Andel's Singer. They were sprawled on the ground around the grotto, unconscious.

Kassandra crossed her arms in front of her, shaking her head when Merry asked Ellen to see if she could wake them up. 'We should leave them here. They will wake up eventually and still be oath bound to obey Lord Andel, or Karl.'

'Merry transmuted the heartstones binding their oaths into a firestone,' said Gabriel. 'That could have freed them.'

'Lord Andel said the oaths could never be broken, except by using another heartstone, and I'm pretty sure none of you would volunteer yours. I certainly wouldn't weaken myself if I had one.' Kassandra raised an eyebrow.

She was right. Merry couldn't give up her heartstone, and for Ellen to do so would mean a lessening of her healing ability. And even if Gabriel was willing, he had only one and there were six mages.

'Unless you can get your hands on a stash of heart-stones, and a Spirit mage who knows how to break oaths,' Kassandra added, 'these mages belong to Andel and Karl. We could never trust them not to stab us in the back.'

'Gabriel is right though,' said Ellen, 'Merry trans-muting the heartstones could have voided the oaths made on them, but we will never know if we don't try.' She knelt beside one of the Fire mages. 'And we can't just leave them like this. From what I sense, he is in a deep coma and is unlikely to ever wake without inter-vention. They will die if I don't help them.' Concern throbbed in her voice, and yet she made no move to heal them. Instead she eyed Merry, waiting for her response.

'We need to wake at least one of them up to find out

what happened to the enforcers guarding them,' said Adrian, with a bleak expression.

Merry grimaced at the thought they might have also been oath bound against their will. But if they were anything like him, they would not have abandoned their charges for any other reason.

With a sigh, she said, 'We have to take the risk. Whether they are still oath bound or not, we can't just walk away and let them die. If we do that, we're no better than Andel.'

With a relieved smile, Ellen placed a hand on the mage's forehead and clasped her heartstone with the other.

As the healer's spell worked, colour returned to the mage's face and his breathing sped up. His eyelashes fluttered and he gave a groan, one hand lifting to rub at his temple. Merry tensed as he removed the hand and turned his head to look directly at her, anger in his gaze.

Was he about to attack?

She readied herself to fight, but the mage shifted his gaze to glare at the others, his expression darkening even further when he spotted Adrian. 'Enforcer Irvine, what is the meaning of this? Have you turned traitor?'

Adrian stiffened. 'Master Regis, I am loyal to the guild.'

'Then why are you doing nothing to apprehend these traitors?' The mage shifted to a sitting position, one hand bracing himself upright while the other waved towards the five mages who were still comatose. 'You stand there, doing nothing, after these fiends have attacked me and my fellow mages.'

'We didn't attack anyone. This was the work of Lord Andel and his rebels,' said Merry, glaring down at him. 'We're trying to help you.'

Regis' brow furrowed. 'Lord Andel?'

Ellen leaned forward, once again placing a hand on his forehead. 'What is the last thing you remember?'

'We were attempting to stabilise the Fire focal point, but it was beyond our control.' He shook his head, expression bleak. 'The best we could do was contain it to give the people of Haven more time to flee.'

He looked over at the grotto and his eyes widened. 'We succeeded?' He scrambled to his feet and approached the flickering flame, holding his hands towards it. 'But how? It was at flashpoint. We should all be dead now.' He swung back to face them. 'What did we do?'

'It wasn't you,' said Gabriel, pushing forward. 'It was Merry.'

Regis snorted. 'Impossible. She is no Fire mage. How could she achieve something six of us together could not do?'

'Impossible or not, Merry saved us all. But that is not all that happened.' Gabriel explained how Regis and the others had been subverted by Lord Andel's people.

From the expression on his face, Regis didn't believe this any more than he believed that Merry had been responsible for calming the Fire focal point. He was so rigid in his thinking; he could never understand how someone could become one with the element. For him, it was all about controlling the Fire. But in surrendering to it, Merry had been able to achieve the impossible, even if she had almost lost her sense of self in the process.

Arms crossed in front of him, Regis glared at Gabriel. 'I feel no different, and I have no memory of anything you say took place here. There is no way I was under someone else's control.'

Merry turned to Donna. 'Can you tell if he is telling the truth?'

'I am no liar, girl.' Regis backed up as Donna moved towards him. 'And there is no way I am letting this traitor anywhere near me.'

Donna gave a dark chuckle. 'You don't have a choice.'

Goosebumps rippled over Merry's skin as the Spirit mage waved her hand. Regis stiffened, eyes wide and unseeing as Donna closed in and placed a hand on his forehead.

A moment later, she stepped back and faced Merry, while Regis remained as he was. 'He's been oath bound, but there are gaps in his memory that appear to be deliberate. I can't see what transpired here, or what the terms of the oath were, but someone has gone to the trouble of ensuring he does not remember.'

Damn. There went the faint hope that transmuting the heartstones would have freed them from their oaths. Not that it would have been an easy task. It had taken the might of the Fire focal point to allow Merry to turn six of them into a firestone. She would just have to hope the Singers would have a way to free Tara and all the others who had unwillingly been bound up in Lord Andel's bid for the throne.

But that was a problem for another time. Right now Merry had to focus on the one right in front of her. 'So he would return to the guild, with no idea he had been subverted.'

'Indeed.' Donna moved to kneel beside one of the other mages. 'This one is the same, and I suspect the others will have been tampered with also.'

'So they're basically ticking time bombs, unaware they could go off at any second.' Merry shook her head. The amount of damage six Fire mages could do would be catastrophic.

Ellen blanched. 'They'll die if I don't wake them up.'

'No one said anything about not waking them,' said Gabriel. 'We just need to be prepared.' He turned to Adrian. 'Will you be able to manage them?'

Adrian gave a slow nod. 'I'll keep a close eye on them as we head back to the tower, and I'll send word ahead, so Mage Fairweather is aware they have been compromised.'

'You're not coming with us?' Ellen's gaze darkened.

'I can't, no matter how much I might wish it were otherwise. My oath is to protect the guild, and its mages. I have to make sure this lot don't cause trouble until they can be neutralised.' His jaw clenched. 'I also need to find out what happened to Branstone and the others. Mage Fairweather needs to be informed of the possibility that they may have been turned.'

'Do you think she'll believe you, once she finds out we were involved?' Merry didn't think Ophelia Fairweather would trust Donna's word on her mages being compromised, even if she wasn't bespelled by the guild heartstone. The guild leader was unlikely to believe anyone who had fought alongside Meredith Meadows.

If Ophelia knew Adrian had worked around his oath to help her and Gabriel, he was likely to end up locked in the tower with Tara.

Adrian's lips twitched into a grim smile. 'I'm not stupid. I wasn't planning on revealing your role in this until after Mage Fairweather has confirmed Mage Syphera's diagnosis.'

'Smart.' Merry returned his smile and then turned to Donna. 'Can you make sure Mage Regis can't remember any of this?'

'It is a simple matter to create a memory block,' said Donna, as she kneeled beside the Fire mage.

While the Spirit mage worked, Merry turned to Ellen. 'Is there a way you can get them to wake up after we leave? The less brain scrambling Donna has to do the better.'

Ellen gave a quick nod and then set to work on the remaining five comatose Fire mages, while Donna worked on Regis for a few moments. When both Ellen and Donna indicated they were ready, Merry and her friends headed for the exit.

'You will need supplies,' said Adrian. 'The Haven mayor ensured we were well provisioned before he joined the evacuation. You can take what you need. I'd give you one of the wagons, but its loss would be hard to explain to Mage Regis and the others.'

'Thank you, my friend, for all your help. I know it cannot have been easy for you, to resist the constraints of your oath.'

Adrian grimaced. 'It is a small discomfort to bear, given the consequences.'

Merry did not envy his task. With no way of knowing what commands had been imbedded in the Fire mages, and no idea what had happened to his fellow enforcers, it would be a nerve-racking trip.

Not that she and her friends wouldn't have their own problems to deal with. Her senses could find no sign of the black-haired Singer or the magic users that had been with him. While she would like to think it was because they had fled the area and she would never see any of them again, she knew she wasn't that lucky. With the Fire focal point having not gone ballistic, they would know their plan had failed. They would also know where Merry was headed next; back to the guild tower to get her Spirit charm.

Talk about nerve-racking trips. The guild would still be on the lookout for her too and while Adrian had been able to work around his oath, he would eventually have to come clean about what had taken place here. She glanced over at the enforcer as he led them towards the clearing where the guild mages had set up camp. He'd talked about discomfort, but he showed no signs of the pain and distress Tara had experienced when she'd been stopped from leading Merry into a trap back at the guild tower.

Maybe the oath to obey guild law was not as strong as the ones unwillingly bound by Andel's rogue Singer. Kassandra was certainly able to operate around the oath, though it had stopped her from hurting Merry when Karl had commanded it. Whatever the reason, she was thankful Adrian was on their side.

Leaving the Fire mages lying on the sand in the grotto, they followed the main path back towards the clearing around the sundial. A short distance from it, Adrian called a halt and turned to Merry.

'Can you sense any of my enforcers in the camp?'

Merry had been scanning for threats from the moment they exited the tunnel and the hope in his eyes dimmed when she shook her head. 'I'm sorry.' She might not be fond of his enforcers, particularly Branstone, but she could understand Adrian's concern for his comrades.

His jaw clenched and he gave a sharp nod. 'In that case, it should be safe for you to enter the camp to collect what supplies you need to get you to the tower.'

Gabriel clasped the enforcer on the shoulder. 'Thank you, my friend.'

They walked the short distance to the camp, and Merry's stomach lurched at finding it in disarray. The grass was churned up and belongings scattered everywhere. There was no sign of people present, or of the horses that had pulled the wagons, one of which was overturned and its contents spilled onto the ground.

Adrian's expression darkened as he took in the sight.

Gabriel pointed towards scuff marks in the dirt. 'There are horse tracks leading this way. I will conduct a search, while you and the others salvage what you can,' he said to Merry. 'I won't be long.'

'I will help you,' said Adrian, and the two of them strode off, with Beethoven on their heels, soon disappearing within the trees.

Merry worked alongside Ellen, and together they looked for any food suitable for a journey, and placed it in a pack, while Donna and Kassandra rummaged through the rest of the supplies for anything useful. After a few minutes, they had everything they planned to take with them neatly piled up. Adrian and Gabriel had not returned with the horses, and Merry scanned the gap in the trees where they had entered the forest. Ellen was also peering in that direction, brow furrowed.

'I thought they would have returned by now,' said Ellen.

'Same,' said Merry as she stretched out her senses to search for Gabriel and Adrian.

There was no sign of the runaway horses, or the two men who had gone to collect them. She ranged farther and farther, finding an empty forest, not even the spark of small animals registering to her Earth sense.

'Merry.' Concern thrummed in Ellen's voice. 'Have you found them?'

Cold dread set in as Merry turned to her friend and shook her head. 'I can't sense them at all.'

I am unable to contact Beethoven. Sadie moved closer to the tree-line. *I will search for them and show you what I find.*

'Sadie, no.' Merry darted in front of the cat. 'It's not safe. I don't want to lose you too. They can't have just vanished without reason. The forest is too quiet. It's not natural.'

'Merry is right. Whatever is happening is not natural. My magic tells me the forest is devoid of life, yet that is not possible.' Donna stepped up beside Merry, Kassandra at her back.

'It's an invisibility shield,' said Merry, 'like the one they used at the volcano.' That shield had taken dozens of magic users to create. She gazed warily at the seemingly dead forest. Its shadowy interior could hold any number of enemies, with the shield to hide behind.

'We need to flee, now,' said Kassandra.

'We can't leave until we find Adrian and Gabriel,' said Ellen.

Merry hated the thought of leaving them behind, but Kassandra was right. They couldn't just stand there and wait for whatever trap had caught the others to snap closed on them as well.

Still keeping an ear on the forest, she placed a hand on Ellen's arm. 'We're not leaving them; we're finding a better place to fight. We need to retreat to Haven, and then we can figure out what to do next.' The clearing they were in offered limited cover, and had not served the enforcers well, so she hoped the town's walls would offer better protection.

When Ellen gave a reluctant nod, Merry hefted her pack and gripped her staff tightly. The others grabbed packs as well, leaving Gabriel's behind. They would retrieve it after they were reunited.

If they were reunited.

No, she couldn't think like that. Gabriel had been a staunch ally from the moment they had found each other in the Cavern of Heart Songs. He was a welcome friend, who had gone against his aunt to aid Merry in her quest. She would find him again. She would save him and Beethoven, and Adrian, from whatever trap they had been caught in.

No one spoke as they hurried along the path leading back to Haven. Merry's tension grew with each step, her certainty that they would be attacked without warning growing. It was only a small relief to reach the corner of the town walls. Now they had to worry about an attack on only three sides.

They reached the open town gates without incident, and Merry called a halt as she once again probed Haven with her senses. As with the forest, there was no sign of human life, but the sparks of small animals and other creatures reassured her no one was using an invisibility shield to lie in wait. She ushered her friends through the gate while she sent her probe back the way they had come.

A faint spark at the edge of her reach pinged her senses, too small to be a person.

Merry, wait.

The mental cry was faint, threaded through with pain, but there was no mistaking who it belonged to.

'Beethoven.' Merry dropped her pack and raced back along the path, her awareness of the grey and white familiar increasing with each step. She heard the others running along behind her, even as a black streak dodged around Merry and darted ahead as the stumbling figure of Beethoven appeared on the path.

Sadie reached the other cat first, just as he toppled sideways. The black cat bent down and nudged his head. *He is badly injured.*

Merry's heart thudded as she sprinted the rest of the way and saw Beethoven's silky fur coated in blood and dirt clinging to his face.

'Merry, get the healing herbs from my pack and add some to the water skin,' said Ellen as she knelt beside Beethoven. One hand was on her heartstone as she reached out the other and laid it gently on the familiar's injured side.

Merry's hands trembled as she followed Ellen's instructions. Beethoven was so still, not making a sound as the healer ministered to his wounds, but she could hear his anguish in his mental cries.

Gabriel is gone. I can't find him.

'Shush, it's okay, we will get him back.' Merry handed the canteen to Ellen and then gently stroked Beethoven's head as the healer did her spell to invigorate the water.

She moved aside so Ellen could coax the cat to drink. Little by little, the cat lapped at the healing water in the healer's palm. The wound on his side was now closed, though the fur around it remained stained with his blood. Once he had drunk his fill, Ellen used more water to wash his side.

With a mental wince, Beethoven got to his feet and sniffed at the scar that remained. He nudged up against Ellen. *I thank you for your kind attention.*

Then he turned to face Merry. *They lay in wait for us, hidden among the horses. Gabriel fought bravely as did Enforcer Irvine, but the rogue Singer used his perverted heartstones to bind them to his will. I tried to save them both, but there were too many of them. I was struck, and one of the magic users with him cast a spell that rendered me unconscious. When I woke, they were gone.*

He hung his head. *I failed him.*

Before Merry could protest, Sadie reached out a paw and swatted Beethoven on his head. *Stop being so melodramatic. There is no time to wallow in self-pity. Your mage is in trouble, and it is up to us to get him out of it.*

Beethoven stiffened at her words, arching his back

and narrowing his green eyes. *I will make them rue this day.*

Sadie sat on her haunches, a pleased vibe coming through with her mental voice. *WE will make them rue daring to come between a companion and his mage.*

Beethoven blinked once, at her terming him a companion and not a familiar. Then he inclined his head. *Indeed, we will.*

Then both cats turned to face Merry, waiting for her to announce their next step.

It was imperative that she reached the guild tower as soon as possible, to get her last charm. That would mean leaving Gabriel and Adrian in the hands of the Singer who now had total control of their abilities.

She had told Britta that freeing Tara from thrall would have to wait until after they had secured the portal to Merry's world. That they would never be able to trust her daughter would not turn on them against her will. It has seemed so sensible then, to delay rescuing Tara until they were better equipped to break the oath that bound her to Lord Andel's cause.

But this was Gabriel; the man who had fought at her side so many times, unashamedly allowing her to see how much he cared for her when they had linked to destroy the poison stone in Marshland. The memory of his kiss still burned, and Merry regretted not taking the time to explore the depths of his feelings for her, and hers for him once they had escaped the guild tower.

Eyes prickling with unshed tears, and a bitter taste in

her mouth, Merry shook her head. 'It would take a week of travelling for us to reach the Singers. Even if I can convince Alicia to break the oaths the rogue Singer has made, we would then need to find Gabriel, and Adrian, to free them. Winter is almost here, and I have to get my Spirit charm so we can stop the witch hunters from using the portal. Then, when Tirana is safe, we can rescue our friends, and everyone else that has been enslaved.'

Silence met her words.

After a long moment, Ellen took a deep breath and then exhaled slowly. 'Adrian and Gabriel would want us to focus on saving Tirana, though it pains me to think of what they will be forced to do with their will subjugated.'

I do not like this course of action, but I agree with the healer. This is what Gabriel would want us to do. Beethoven fixed his green gaze on Merry. *As soon as we have secured Tirana against witch hunters, we will rescue him.*

Merry gave a nod, and then turned to the others. Donna and Kassandra both nodded, while Sadie mentally voiced her agreement.

A lump in her throat made it impossible for Merry to speak, though there were no words to describe how awful it felt to be abandoning Gabriel and Adrian to their uncertain fate. Instead, she gripped her staff tightly and strode the short distance back to where they had dropped their packs.

Her pace sped up with each step.

The sooner she got her hands on her Spirit charm, and made the transportation spell, the better. Nothing would stand in her way. Not the mages and enforcers in the tower perched above the Spirit focal point. Not the lord who wanted to be a king or the rogue Singer who had stolen her friends.

She would succeed in stopping the witch hunters. Then she would not rest until she had freed every single witch, mage or enforcer who had been oath bound against their will, starting with Gabriel Fairweather.

ALSO BY SHELLEY RUSSELL NOLAN

Merry Magic

Spell Struck

Spell Shock

Spell Stone

Spell Search

The Last Ward

Dark Justice

Dark Vengeance

Dark Allegiance

Reaper's Ascension Series

Outcast Reaper

Lost Reaper

Winged Reaper

Silver Reaper

Arcane Awakenings Novella Series

Arcane Awakenings Books One and Two

Arcane Awakenings Books Three and Four

Arcane Awakenings Books Five and Six

ACKNOWLEDGMENTS

Writing a book and getting it published is not always easy. This book, in particular, has been a hard journey. The last year has been a difficult one, for many reasons, and my creative energy took a hit. For a while there it seemed like Spell Search would never be finished. Thanks to my wonderful family and a super supportive bunch of friends and fellow authors, I finally got to write 'The End.'

Of course, this is not the end of Merry's adventures, with two more books to come before her story is complete. I promise it won't take me so long to get those books written. In the meantime, I would like to take this opportunity to thank Pixie Covers for the amazing cover, and Sally Odgers for her editing prowess and making my story shine.

Also, thank you to the readers who have been patiently waiting for Merry's next adventure to be released. I hope you enjoy it.

ABOUT THE AUTHOR

Shelley Russell Nolan is an avid reader who began writing her own stories at sixteen. Her first completed manuscript featured brain eating aliens and a butt kicking teenage heroine. Since then she has spent her time creating fantasy worlds where death is only the beginning and even freaks can fall in love.

The first two books in her debut adult urban fantasy series, *Lost Reaper* and *Winged Reaper*, were published by Atlas Productions in 2016, with *Silver Reaper* published in 2017 to complete the series. 2018 saw the release of her *Arcane Awakenings Novella Series*, while Odyssey Books published the first book in a new post-apocalyptic series in 2019.

Born in New Zealand, moving to Australia with her family when she was seven, Shelley currently lives in Central Queensland, Australia, with her two young children and two wrecking ball kitties.

Shelley loves to hear from her readers so feel free to contact her on Facebook or leave a review where you purchased this book, on Goodreads or on her website - shelleyrussellnolan.com